William S. Burroughs was born in St Louis, Missouri, in 1914. His many works include *The Naked Lunch* – which made him famous overnight – *Junkie*, *The Soft Machine*, *The Last Words of Dutch Schultz* and *Cities of the Red Night*. In 1983 he was named a Member of the American Academy and Institute of Arts and Letters. Burroughs divides his time between New York City and Lawrence, Kansas.

WILLIAM S. BURROUGHS

The Soft Machine

PALADIN
GRAFTON BOOKS
A Division of the Collins Publishing Group

LONDON GLASGOW
TORONTO SYDNEY AUCKLAND

Paladin
Grafton Books
A Division of the Collins Publishing Group
8 Grafton Street, London W1X 3LA

Published in Paladin Books 1986

This revised edition first published in Great Britain
by Calder & Boyars Ltd 1968
First version published by The Olympia Press, Paris 1961
Second version published by Grove Press, Inc., New York 1966

Copyright © William Burroughs 1961, 1966, 1968

ISBN 0-586-08561-0

Printed and bound in Great Britain by
Collins, Glasgow

Set in Ehrhardt

1

DEAD ON ARRIVAL

I was working the hole with the Sailor and we did not bad fifteen cents on average night boosting the afternoons and short timing the dawn we made out from the land of the free but I was running out of veins ... I went over to the counter for another cup of coffee ... in Joe's Lunch Room drinking coffee with a napkin under the cup which is said to be the mark of someone who does a lot of sitting in cafeterias and lunch rooms ... waiting on the Man ... 'What can we do?' Nick said to me once in his dead junky whisper 'They know we'll wait ...' Yes, they know we'll wait ...

There is a boy sitting at the counter thin-faced kid his eyes all pupil ... I see he is hooked and sick familiar face maybe from the pool hall where I scored for tea sometime somewhere in grey strata of subways all night cafeterias rooming house flesh. His eyes flickered the question. I nodded toward my booth. He carried his coffee over and sat down opposite me.

The croaker lives out Long Island ... light yen sleep waking up for stops.change.start ... everything sharp and clear antennae of TV suck the sky ... The clock jumped ahead the way time will after 4 P.M.

'The Man is three hours late ... You got the bread?'

'I got three cents.'

'Nothing less than a nickel. These double papers he claims' I looked at his face ... good looking ... 'Say kid I know an old auntie croaker write for you like a major ... Take the phone. I don't want him to rumble my voice.'

About this time I meet this Italian Tailor cum Pusher I know from Lexington and he gives me a good buy on H ... At least it was good at first but all the time shorter and shorter ... 'Short Count Tony' we call him ...

Out of junk in East St. Louis sick dawn he threw himself across the wash basin pressing his stomach against the cool porcelain. I draped myself over his body laughing. His shorts dissolved in rectal mucous and carbolic soap. summer dawn smells from a vacant lot.

'I'll wait here ... Don't want him to rumble me ...'

Made it five times under the shower that day soapy bubbles of egg flesh seismic tremors split by fissure spurts of jissom . . .

I made the street, everything sharp and clear like after rain. see Sid in a booth reading a paper his face yellow ivory in the sunlight. I handed him two nickels under the table. Pushing in a small way to keep up the Habit: *invade. damage. occupy.* young faces in blue alcohol flame.

'And use that alcohol. You fucking can't wait hungry junkies all the time black up my spoons. That's all I need for Pen Indef the fuzz rumbles a black spoon in my trap.' The old junky spiel. Junk hooks falling.

'Shoot your way to freedom kid.'

Trace a line of goose pimples up the thin young arm. Slide the needle in and push the bulb watching the junk hit him all over. Move right in with the shit and suck junk through all the hungry young cells.

There is a boy sitting like your body. I see he is a hook. I drape myself over him from the pool hall. draped myself over his cafeteria and his shorts dissolved in strata of subways . . . and all house flesh . . . toward the booth . . . down opposite me . . . The Man an Italian tailor . . . I know bread. 'Me a good buy on H.'

'You're quitting? Well I hope you make it, kid. May I fall down and be paralyzed if I don't mean it . . . You gotta friend in me. a real friend and if . . .'

Well the traffic builds up and boosters falling in with jackets shirts and ties, kids with a radio torn from the living car trailing tubes and wires, lush-workers flash rings and wrist watches falling in sick all hours. I had the janitor cooled, an old rummy, but it couldn't last with that crowd.

'Say you're looking great kid. Now do yourself a favour and stay off. I been getting some really great shit lately. Remember that brown shit sorta yellow like snuff cooks up brown and clear . . .'

Junky in East bath room . . . invisible and persistent dream body . . . familiar face maybe . . . scored for some time or body . . . in that grey smell of rectal mucous . . . night cafeterias and junky room dawn smells. three hours from Lexington made it five times . . . soapy egg flesh . . .

'These double papers he claims of withdrawal.'

'Well I thought you was quitting . . .'

'I can't make it.'

'Impossíble quitàr eso.'

Got up and fixed in the sick dawn flutes of Ramadan.

'William tu tomas mas medicína? ... No me hégas caso, William.'

Casbah house in the smell of dust and we made it; empty Eukodal boxes stacked four feet along the walls ... dead on the surplus blankets ... girl screaming ... Vecinos rush in ...

'What did she die of?'

'I don't know she just died.'

Bill Gains in Mexico City room with his douche bag and his stash of codeine pills powdered in a bicarbonate can; 'I'll just say I suffer from indigestion.' coffee and blood spilled all over the place. cigarette holes in the pink blanket ... The Consul would give me no information other than place of burial in the American Cemetery.

'Broke? Have you no pride? Go to your Consul.' He gave me an alarm clock ran for a year after his death.

Leif repatriated by the Danish. Freight boat out of Casa for Copenhagen sank off England with all hands. Remember my medium of distant fingers? –

'What did she die of?'

'End.'

'Some things I find myself.'

The Sailor went wrong in the end. Hanged to a cell door by his principals: 'Some things I find myself doing I'll pack in is all.'

bread knife in the heart ... rub and die ... repatriated by a morphine script ... those out of Casa for Copenhagen on special yellow note ...

'All hands broke? Have you no pride?' Alarm clock ran for a year. 'He just sit down on the curb and die.' Esperanza told me on Niño Perdido and we cashed a morphine script. those Mexican Nar. scripts on special yellow bank-note paper ... like a thousand dollar bill ... or a Dishonorable Discharge from the US Army ... and fixed in the cubicle room you reach by climbing this ladder.

yesterday call flutes of Ramadan: 'No me hágas cáso.'

Blood spills over shirts and light. The American trailing in form ... He went to Madrid. This frantic Cuban fruit finds Kiki with a novia and stabs him with a kitchen knife in the heart. (Girl screaming. Enter the nabors.)

'Quédase con su medicína, William.'

Half bottle of Fundador after half cure in the Jew Hospital. shots of demerol by candle light. They turned off the lights and water. paper-like dust we made it. empty walls. Look anywhere. No good. No bueno.

He went to Madrid ... Alarm clock ran for yesterday ... 'No me hágas cáso.' dead on arrival ... you might say at the Jew Hospital ... blood spilled over the American ... trailing lights and water ... The Sailor went so wrong somewhere in that grey flesh ... He just sit down on zero ... I nodded on Niño Perdido his coffee over three hours late ... They all went away and sent papers ... The Dead Man write for you like a major ... Enter vecinos ... Freight boat smell of rectal mucous went down off England with all dawn smell of distant fingers ... About this time I went to your Consul. He gave me a Mexican after his death ... Five times of dust we made it ... with soap bubbles of withdrawal crossed by a thousand junky nights ... Soon after the half maps came in by candlelight ... *Occupy* ... Junk lines falling ... Stay Off ... Bill Gains in the Yellow Sickness ... looking at dirty pictures casual as a ceiling fan short-timing the dawn we made it in the corn smell of rectal mucous and carbolic soap ... familiar face maybe from the vacant lot ... trailing tubes and wires ... 'You fucking-can't-wait-hungry-junkies! ...' burial in the American Cemetery. 'Quédase con su medicína' ... on Niño Perdido the girl screaming ... They all went way through Casbah House ... 'Couldn't your write me any better than that? Gone away ... You can look anyplace.'

No good. No Bueno.

2
WHO AM I TO BE CRITICAL?

You wouldn't believe how hot things were when I left the States – I knew this one pusher wouldn't carry any shit on his person just shoot it in the line – ten twenty grains over and above his own absorption according to the route he was servicing and piss it out in bottles for his customers so if the heat came up on them they cop out as degenerates – So Doc Benway assessed the situation and came up with this brain child

'Once in the Upper Baboonasshole I was stung by a scorpion – the sensation is not dissimilar to a fix-Hummm.'

So he imports this special breed of scorpions and feeds them on metal meal and the scorpions turned a phosphorescent blue color and sort of hummed 'Now we must find a worthy vessel' he said – So we flush out this old goof ball artist and put the scorpion to him and he turned sort of blue and you could see he was fixed right to metal – These scorpions could travel on a radar beam and service the clients after Doc coped for the bread – It was a good thing while it lasted and the heat couldn't touch us – However all these scorpion junkies began to glow in the dark and if they didn't score on the hour metamorphosized into scorpions straight away – So there was a spot of bother and we had to move on disguised as young junkies on the way to Lexington – Bill and Johnny we sorted out the names but they keep changing like one day I would wake up as Bill the next day as Johnny – So there we are in the train compartment shivering junk sick our eyes watering and burning and all of a sudden the sex chucks hit me in the crotch and I sagged against the wall and looked at Johnny too weak to say anything it wasn't necessary he was there too and without a word he dipped some soap in warm water and dropped my shorts and rubbed the soap on my ass and worked his cock up me with a cockscrew motion and we both came right away standing there and swaying with the train clickety clack clack spurt spurt into the brass cuspidor – We never got to Lexington actually – Stopped off in the town of Marshal and hit this old country croaker for tincture with the aged mother suffering from piles in the worst form there is line and he wrote like a major – That night we got into a pool game and Doc won a Dussenberg Panama hat and a tan, and dark glasses like 1920 sports and the further South we went the easier it was to score like we brought the '20s along with us – Well we come to this Mexican border town in time to see something interesting – In order to make way for a new bridge that never got built actually they had torn down a block of shacks along the river where the chink railway workers used to smoke the black stuff and the rats had been down under the shacks hooked for generations – So the rats was running all through the street squealing sick biting everyone in sight –

When we went to look for our car couldn't find it and no cars anywhere just this train left over from an old Western – The track gave out somewhere north of Monterrey and we bought some horses off a chinaman for a tin of mud – By this time there were soldiers everywhere shooting the civilians so we scored for some civil war uniforms and joined one of the warring powers – And captured five soldiers who were wearing uniforms of a different color and the General got drunk and decided to hang the prisoners just for jolly and we rigged up a cart with a drop under a tree limb – The first one dropped straight and clean and one of the soldiers wiped his mouth and stepped forward grinning and pulled his pants down to an ankle and his cock flipped spurting – We all stood there watching and feeling it right down to our toes and the others who were waiting to be hanged felt it too – That night we requisitioned a ranch house and all got drunk and Johnny did this dance with his tie around his neck lolling his head on one side and letting his tongue fall out and wriggled his ass and dropped his pants and his cock flipped out and the soldiers rolled around laughing till they pissed all over themselves – Then they rigged up a harness under his arms and hoisted him up off the floor to a beam and gang fucked him –

By the time we got to Monterrey there was Spaniards around in armour like a costume movie and again we were lucky to arrive just at the right time. There was a crowd of people in the Zoco and we pushed up front with our rush hour technique and saw they were getting ready to burn some character at the stake – When they lit the faggots at his feet the only sound you could hear was the fire crackling and then everyone sucked in his breath together and the screams tore through me and my lips and tongue swole up with blood and I come in my pants – And I could see others had shot their load too and you could smell it like a compost heap some of us so close our pants steamed in the fire just pulling the screams and the smoke down into our lungs and sort of whimpering – It was tasty I tell you. So we hit Mexico city just before sunrise and I said here we go again – That heart pulsing in the sun and my cock pulsed right with it and jissom seeped through my thin cotton trousers and fell in the dust and shit of the street – And a boy next to me grinning and gave me a back hand pick pocket feel my cock still hard and aching like after a wet dream – And we crawled up onto a muddy shelf by the canal and made it there three times slow fuck on knees in the stink of sewage looking at the black water – It turned out later this kid had the epilepsy – When he got these fits he would flop around and come maybe five times in his dry goods made you feel good all over to watch it – He really had it built in and he told me he could fix it with a magic man we trade places – So we started off on foot across the mountains and down the other side to high jungle warm and steamy and he kept having these fits and I dug it special fucking him in the spasm his ass hole fluttering like a vibrator – Well we come to this village and found the magic man in a little hut on the outskirts – and evil old character with sugary eyes that stuck to you – We told him what we wanted and he nodded and looked at both of us and smiled and said he would have to cook up the medicine we should come back next day at sun down – So we came back and he gave us the bitter medicine in clay pots – And I hadn't put the pot down before the pictures started coming in sharp and clear: the hanged boy pulling his legs up to the chin and pumping out the spurts by the irrigation ditch, the soldiers swinging me around in the harness, the burned man screaming away like a good one and that heart just pulsing and throwing off spurts or blood in the rising sun – Xolotl was explaining to me that only one body is left in the switch they were going to hang me and when I shot my load and died I would pass into his body – I was paralyzed by the medicine any case and they stripped me and lashed my body with special type sex nettles that burned and stung all over and my tongue swole up and gagged me and my eyes blurred over with blood – They rigged up a gallows with a split bamboo platform and a ladder and I start up the ladder Xolotl goosing me and stood under the noose and he tightens it around my neck muttering spells and then gets down on the floor leaving me along up there on the platform with the noose waiting – I saw him reach up with a obsidian knife and cut the rope held the platform and I fell and silver light popped in my eyes like a flash bulb – I got a whiff of ozone and penny arcades and then I felt it start way down in my toes these bone wrenching spasms emptied me and everything spilled out shit running down the back of my thighs and no control in my body paralyzed, twisting up in these spasms the jissom just siphoned me right into Xolotl's cock and next thing I was in his ass and balls flopping around spurting all over the floor and that evil old fuck crooning and running his hands over me so nasty – But then who am I to be critical? – I stayed there in the magic man's hut for three days sleeping and woke up the look out different – And the magic man gave me some medicine to control the fits and I headed on south – Came at sun down to a clear river where boys were swimming naked – And one of them turned grinning with a hard on and shoved his finger in and out his fist and I fell in one of my fits so they all had a go at me – The cold mountain shadows came down and touched my naked ass and I went back with the boy to his hut and ate beans and chili and lay with him on the floor breathing the pepper smell of his belches and stayed there with him and worked his patch of corn on the side of the mountain – That boy could keep a hard on all night and I used to stick peppers up my ass when he fucked me like my guts was on fire – Well maybe I would be there still work all day and after the work knocked out no words no thoughts just sit there looking at the blue mountains and ate and belched and fucked and slept same thing day after day the greatest – But one day we scored for a bottle of mezcal and got lushed and he looked at me and said:

'Chingoa de puto I will rid the earth of you in the name of Jesus Christu!'

and charges me with a machete – Well I'd seen it coming and tossed a cup of mezcal in his eyes and side stepped and he fell on his face and I rammed the planting stick right into the base of his brain – So that was that – And started South again and came finally to this spot where a lot of citizens were planting corn with sticks all working in concert I didn't like the look of it but I was strung out for groceries and decided to make contact a mistake as it turned out – Because as soon as I walked out into that field I felt this terrible weight on me and there I was planting corn with them and everything I did and thought was already done and thought and there was this round of festivals where the priests put on lobster suits and danced around snapping their claws like castanets and nothing but maize maize maize – And I guess I would be there yet frutifying the maize God except for this one cat who was in Maya drag like me but I could see he was a foreigner too – He was very technical and a lovely fellow – He began drawing formulae on the floor and showed me how the priests operated their control racket 'It's like with the festivals and the fucking corn they know what everybody will see and hear and smell and taste and that's what thought is and these thought units are represented by symbols in their books and they rotate the symbols around and around on the calendar' And as I looked at his formulaes something began to crack up in my brain and I was free of the control beam and next thing we both got busted and sentenced to 'Death In Centipede' – So they strapped us to couches in a room under the temple and there was a terrible smell in the place full of old bones and a centipede about ten feet long comes nuzzling out of one corner – So I turn on something I inherit from Uranus where my grandfather invented the adding machine – I just lay there without any thought in tons focus of heavy blue silence and a slow wave went through me and spread out of me and the couch began shaking and the tremors spread into the ground and the roof fell in and crushed the centipede and smashed the couch so the straps were loose and I slipped out and untied Technical Tilly – So we got out of there dodging stellae and limestone skulls as the whole temple came down in chunks and the wind blowing a hurricane brought in a tidal wave and there wasn't much left of the whole set when things cleared away – All the workers were running around loose now looking for the priests – The head priest was paralyzed and had turned into a centipede – We found him in a cubby hole under the rubble along with some others who were half crab or in various stages of disgusting metamorphosis – And I figured we should do something special with these characters they are wise guys – So we organize this 'Fun Fest' and made some obsidian jock straps strung together with copper wire and heated the straps up white hot and slipped them on the priests did a belly dance like you used to see it in burlesque and we sat there yelling: 'Take it off! Take it off!' laughing till we pissed and shit and came – You never heard such laughing with the control gone and goosing them with hot copper pricks – And others we put weights on their backs and dragged them through wooden troughs with flint flakes sticking up and so on – Fun and games what?

Well after that none of us could look at corn and the grocery problem became acute – So we organize this protection racket

13

shaking down the agriculturals – 'It could happen again here – Kick in or else' – And they kicked in come level on average – Well groceries – And I had perfected a gimmick to keep my boys in line – I was still subject to these fits but I had learned to control the images – That is just before I flipped out I could put any image in the projector and – Action – Camera – Take – It always happened the way I took it and any character gave me any static was taken care of that way – But the boys from the North were moving in whole armies so we packed in and shifted to the hunting and fishing lark – I picked thirty of the most likely and suitable lads all things considered and we moved South up over the mountains and down the other side into jungle then up and over again getting monotonous – piecing out the odds best we could spot of this and a spot of that – Once in a while I had to put it about with the earthquakes but come level on average what you might call a journeyman thief – well fever and snakes and rapids and boys dropping out here and there to settle down with the locals I had no mob left when I run up against this really evil set up – The Chimu were something else – So we hit this town and right away I don't like it

'Something here, John – Something wrong – I can feel it'

To begin with the average Chimu is unappetising to say the least – lips eaten off by purple and orange skin conditions like a baboon's ass and pus seeping out a hole where the nose should be disgust you to see it – and some of them are consisting entirely of penis flesh and subject to blast jissom right out their skull and fold up like an old wine bag – Periodically the Chimu organize fun fests where they choose up sides and beat each other's brains out with clubs and the winning team gang fucks the losers and cut their balls off right after to make pouches for coca leaves they are chewing all the time green spit dripping off them like a cow with the aftosa – All things considered I was not innarrested to contact their loutish way of life –

In the middle of this town was a construction of clay cubicles several stories high and I could see some kinda awful crabs were stirring around inside it but couldn't get close because the area around the cubicle is covered with black bones and hot as a blast furnace – They had this heat weapon you got it? – Like white hot ants all over you –

Meanwhile I had been approached by the green boys have a whole whore house section built on cat walks over the mud flats entirely given over to hanging and all kinds death in orgasm young boys need it special – They were beautiful critters and swarmed all over me night and day smelling like a compost heap – But I wasn't buying it sight unseen and when I proposed to watch a hanging they come on all indignant like insulted whores – So I am rigged up a long distance periscope with obsidian mirrors Technical Tilly moaning about the equipment the way he always does and we watched them hang this boy just down from the country – Well I saw that when his neck snapped and he shot his load instead of flowing into the green boy the way nature intended these hot crabs hatched out of his spine and scoffed the lot.

So we organize the jungle tribes and take Boy's Town and confine the green boys in a dormitory, they are all in there turning cartwheels and giggling and masturbating and playing flutes – That was our first move to cut the supply line – Then after we had put the squeeze on and you could hear them scratching around in the cubicle really thin now we decided to attack – I had this special green boy I was making it with who knew the ropes you might say and he told me we have to tune the heat wave out with music – So we get all the Indians and all the green boys with drums and flutes and copper plates and stayed just out of the heat blast beating the drums and slowly closed in – Technical Tilly had rigged up a catapult to throw limestone boulders and shattered the cubicle so we move in with spears and clubs and finish them off and smashed the heat sending set that was a living radio with insect parts – We turn the green boys loose and on our way rejoicing –

So down into the jungle on the head shrinking lark – Know how it operates You got these spells see? confines the citizen to his head under your control like you can shrink up all the hate in the area – What a gimmick but as usual I got greedy and the wind up is I don't have a head left to stand on – Sure I had the area sewed up but there wasn't any area left – Always was one to run things into the ground – Well there I was on the bottom when I hear about this virgin tribe called the Camuyas embrace every stranger and go naked all the time like nature intended and I said 'the Camuyas are live ones' and got down there past all these burocrats with the Internal Indian Service doubted the purity of my intentions – But I confounded them with my knowledge of Mayan archaeology and the secret meaning of the centipede motif and Iam was very technical so we establish ourselves as scientists and got the safe conduct – Those Camuyas were something else all naked rubbing up against you like dogs and I might be there still except for a spot of bother with the Indian Commission about this hanging ceremony I organize figuring to trade in the chassis and renew my substance – So they chucked me out and talked usefully about that was that – And I made it up to the Auca who were war-like and wangled two healthy youths for a secret weapon – So took these boys out into the jungle and laid it on the line and one of them was ready to play ball and – Spare you the monotonous details – Suffice it to say the Upper Amazon gained a hustler and there I was caught in the middle of all these feuds – Some one knocks off your cousin twice removed and you are obligated to take care of his great uncle – Been through all this before – Every citizen you knock off there are ten out looking for you geometric and I don't want to know – So I got a job with the Total Oil Company and that was another mistake –

Rats was running all over the morning – Somewhere North of Monterrey went into the cocaine business – by this time fish tail Cadillac – people – civilians – So we score for some business and get rich over the warring powers – shady or legitimate the same fuck of a different color and the general on about the treasure – We rigged their stupid tree limb and drop the alien corn – spot of business to Wallgreens – So we organize this 8267 kicked in level on average ape – melodious gimmick to keep the boys in line – I had learned to control Law 334 procuring an orgasm by any image, Mary sucking him and running the outfield – Static was taken care of that way – what you might call a vending machine and boys dropping to Wallgreens – We are not locals. We sniff the losers and cut their balls off chewing all kinds masturbation and self abuse like a cow with the aftosa – Young junkies return it to the white reader and one day I would wake up as Bill covered with ice and burning crotch – drop my shorts and comes gibbering up me with a corkscrew motion – We both come right away standing and trying to say something – I see other marks are coming on with the mother tincture – The dogs of Harry J. Anschlinger sprouted all over me – By now we had word dust stirring the 1920s, maze of dirty pictures and the house hooked for generations – We all fucked the boy burglar feeling it right down to our toes – Spanish cock flipped out spurting old Montgomery Ward catalogues – So we stripped a young Dane and rigged the Yankee dollar – Pants down to the ankle, a barefoot Indian stood there watching and feeling his friend – Others had shot their load too over a broken chair through the tool heap – spurts of jissom across the dusty floor – sun rise and I said here we go again with the knife – My cock pulsed right with it and trousers fell in the dust and dead leaves – Return it to the white reader in stink of sewage looking at open shirt flapping and comes maybe five times his ass fluttering like – We sniff what we wanted pumping out the spurts open shirt flapping – What used to be me in my eyes like a flash bulb, spilled adolescent jissom in the bath cubicle – Next thing I was Danny Deaver in Maya drag – That night we requisitioned a Peruvian boy – I would pass into his body – What an awful place it is – most advanced stage – foreigner too – They rotate the symbols around IBM machine with cocaine – Fun and games what?

3

PUBLIC AGENT

So I am a public agent and don't know who I work for, get my instructions from street signs, newspapers and pieces of conversation I snap out of the air the way a vulture will tear entrails from other mouth. In any case I can never catch up on my back cases and currently assigned to intercept blue movies of James Dean before the stuff gets to those queers supporting a James Dean habit which so long as this agent picks his way through barber shops, subway toilets, grope movies and Turkish Baths will never be legal and exempt narcotic.

The first one of the day I nailed in a subway pissoir: 'You fucking nance!' I screamed, 'I'll teach you to savage my bloody meat, I will.' And I sloughed him with the iron glove and his face smashed like rotten canteloupe. Then I hit him in the lungs and blood jumped out his mouth, nose and eyes, spattered three commuters across the room huddled in gabardine topcoats and grey flannel suits under that. The broken fruit was lying with his head damming the piss running over his face and the whole trough a light pink from his blood. I winked at the commuters. 'I can smell them fucking queers,' I sniffed warningly. 'And if there's one thing lower than a nance it's a spot of bloody grass. Now you blokes wouldn't be the type turn around and conger a pal's balls off would you now?' They arranged themselves on the floor like the three monkeys: See No Evil, Hear No Evil, and Speak No Evil.

'I can see you're three of our own,' I said warmly and walked into the corridor where school boys chase each other with machetes, joyous boy-cries and zipper guns echo through the mosaic caverns. I pushed into a Turkish Bath and surprised a faggot brandishing a deformed erection in the steam room and strangled him straight-away with a soapy towel. I had to check in. I was thin now, barely strength in my receding flesh to finish off that tired faggot. I got into my clothes shivering and gaping and walked into the terminal drugstore. Five minutes to twelve. Five minutes to score. I walked over to the night clerk and threw a piece of tin on him.

Piss running over his face. Don't know who I work for. I get mine from his blood new papers and pieces. 'I can smell them fucking the air the way a vulture will.' In any case bloody grass. I sloughed him with the iron room and strangled him like rotten canteloupe. Then I had to check in. I was the blood jumped out his mouth, nose receding flesh to finish. Across the room huddled my clothes shivering grey flannel suits under terminal drugstore. So I am a public agent and the whole trough a light pink instruction from street. I winked at the commuters. 'Conversation I snap out of queers,' I sniffed warningly. 'It's a spot up on my back cases.' Queers supporting the floor like the three monkeys. 'Grope movies and Turkish our own,' I said warmly and walked exempt narcotics. Cool boys chase each other with the first one of the day. to a Turkish bath and surprised you bloody nance. Soapy towel glove hit him in the lungs and eyes spattered: Ping! And walked into the gabardine topcoats. five minutes to that broken fruit.

'Treasury Dept,' I said. 'Like to check your narcotic inventory against RX . . . How much you using young fellow?' Shaking my head and pushing all the junk bottles and scripts into my brief case: 'I hate to see a young man snafu his life script . . . Maybe I can do something for you. That is if you promise me to take the cure and stay off.'

'I promise anything. I gotta wife and kids.'

'Just don't let me down is all.'

I walked out and got straight in the Lu of the Bus Terminal Chinese Restaurant. It's a quiet place with very bad food. but what a John for a junky.

Well I checked into the old Half Moon Hotel you can get to the lobby through the subway and walked in on the wrong room, an ether party, with my cigarette lit and everyone's lungs blew out about six characters, cats and chicks. So I get a face full of tits and spare ribs and throat gristle . . . all in the day's work . . . Follow up on it. Score. I walked the gabardine top tin on him. the broken fruit. piss running over his face. 'Like to check your narcotic inventor. I get mine from his blood.'

'Much you using young fellow?'

'I can smell them fucking all the junk bottles and scripts.' in any case bloody grass . . . See a young man snafu his and strangled him like rot do something for you in the blood. jumped cure and stay off to finish. grey flannel suits under all public agents of the bus from street. grope movie and walked in on the wrong room warmly. exempt light and lungs. and eyes spattered night clerk and threw a piece of coats. 'Five minute to Treasury Department,' I said. shaking my head and pushing the air the way the vulture will into my brief case. I hate sloughed him with the iron room life script. Maybe I can canteloupe. Then I had to check you. Promise me to take out his mouth, nose receding flesh.

'I promise anything. I go huddled my clothes shivering.' I walked out and got light pink instructions terminal Chinese commuters. Hit him in the lungs the day's work. Follow up. A word about my work. The Human Issue has been called in by the Home Office. Engineering flaws you know. There is the work of getting it off the shelves and that is what I do. We are not interested in the individual models, but in the mould, the human die. This must be broken. You never see any live ones up here in Freelandt. Too many patrols. It's a dull territory unless you enjoy shooting a paralyzed swan in a cesspool. Of course there are always the Outsiders. And the young ones I dig special. Long Pigs I call them. Give myself a treat and do it slow just feeding on the subject's hate and fear and the white stuff oozes out when they crack sweet as a lobster claw . . . I hate to put out the eyes because they are my water hole. They call me the Meat Handler. among other things.

I had business with The Egyptian. My Time was running out. He was sitting in a mosaic cafe with stone shelves along the walls and jars of colored syrups sipping a heavy green drink.

'I need the Time Milking,' I said.

He looked at me, his eyes eating erogenous holes. His face got an erection and turned purple. and we went into the vacant lot behind the cafe naked to a turn.

White men killed at a distance. Don't know the answer, do you?

Den Mark of Trak in every face: 'Death, take over.'

'Never nobody liked dancing no better than Red.'

'Let's dance,' he said.

The script for shit, 'Here you are, sir,' and I could see he was heavy with the load. outfields and back to Moscow for Liquidation. I had business with The Gyp. Trak in every kidney. the script for Heavy Drink. His eyes got an erection and turned the effluvia and became addicts of vacant lot. My time was running out its last black grains.

4

TRAK TRAK TRAK

The Sailor and I burned down the Republic of Panama from Darien swamps to David trout streams on paregoric and goof balls – (Note Nembutal) – You lose time putting a con down on a Tiddly Wink chemist – 'No glot – Clom Fliday' – (Footnote: old time junkies will remember – Used to be a lot of Chinese pushers in the 1920s but they found the West so unreliable dishonest and wrong when an Occidental junkie comes to score they say: 'No glot – Clom Fliday.')

And we were running short of Substitute Buyers – They fade in silver mirrors of 1910 under a ceiling fan – Or we lost one at dawn in a wisp of rotten sea wind – Out in the bay little red poison sea snakes swim desperately in sewage – Camphor sweet cooking paregoric smells billow from the mosquito nets – The termite floor gave under our feet spongy and rotten – the albatross at dawn on rusty iron roofs –

'Time to go, Bill,' said the Sailor, morning light on cold coffee

'I'm thin' – criss cross of broken light from wood lathes over the patio, silver flak holes in his face – We worked the Hole together in our lush rolling youth – (Footnote: 'working the Hole', robbing drunks on the subway) – And kicked a habit in East St. Louis – Made it four times third night, fingers scraping bone – at dawn shrinking from flesh and cloth –

Hands empty of hunger on the stale breakfast table – winds of sickness through his face – pain of the long slot burning flesh film – canceled eyes, old photo fading – violet brown souvenir of Panama City – I flew to La Paz trailing the colorless death smell of his sickness with me still, thin air like death in my throat – sharp winds of black dust and the grey felt hat on every head – purple pink and orange disease faces cut prenatal flesh, genitals under the cracked bleeding feet – aching lungs in dust and pain wind – mountain lakes blue and cold as liquid air – indians shitting along the mud walls – brown flesh, red blankets –

'No, senor. Necesita receta.'

And the refugee German croaker you hit anywhere: 'This you must take orally – You will inject it of course – Remember it is better to suffer a month if so you come out – With this habit you lose the life is it not?' And he gives me a long creepy human look –

And Joselito moved in to my room suffocating me with soccer scores – He wore my clothes and we laid the same 'novia' who was thin and sickly always making magic with candles and Virgin pictures and drinking aromatic medicine from a red plastic eye cup and never touched my penis during the sex act.

Through customs checks and control posts and over the mountains in a blue blast of safe conducts and three monkey creatures ran across the road in a warm wind – (sound of barking dogs and running water) swinging round curves over the misty void – down to end of the road towns on the edge of Yage country where shy Indian cops checked our papers – through broken stellae, pottery fragments, worked stones, condoms and shit stained comics, slag heaps of phosphorescent metal excrement – faces eaten by the pink and purple insect disease of the New World – crab boys with human legs and genitals crawl out of clay cubicles – Terminal junkies hawkout crystal throat gristle in the cold mountain wind – Goof ball bums covered with shit sleep in rusty bath tubs – a delta of sewage to the sky under terminal stasis, speared a sick dolphin that surfaced in bubbles of coal gas – taste of metal left silver sores on our lips – only food for this village built on iron racks over an iridescent lagoon – swamp delta to the sky lit by orange gas flares.

In the flash bulb of orgasm I saw three silver numbers – We walked into the streets and won a football pool – Panama clung to our bodies Stranger color through his eyes the look out different

(This sharp smell of carrion)

'Take it from a broken stalemate – The Doctor couldn't reach and see?: Those pictures are the line – Fading breath on bed showed sound track – You win handful of dust that's what.'

metamorphosis of the Rewrite Department coughing and spitting in fractured air – flapping genitals of carrion – Our drained countess passed on a hideous leather body – We are digested and become nothing here – dust air of gymnasiums in another country and besides old the pool now, a few inches on dead post cards – here at the same time there his eyes – Silver light popped stroke of nine.

'Dead post card you got it? – Take it from noon refuse like ash – Hurry up see? – Those pictures *are* yourself – Is backward sound track – That's what walks beside you to a stalemate of physical riders – ("You come with me, Meester?") – I knew Mexican he carried in his flesh with sex acts shooting them pills I took – Total alertness she is your card – Look, simple: Place exploded man goal in other flesh – dual controls country – double sex sad as the drenched lands.'

Last man with such explosion of the throat crawling inexorably from something he carried in his flesh – Last turnstile was in another country and besides knife exploded Sammy The Butcher – holes in 1920 movie – newspaper tape fading, after dinner sleep ebbing carbon dioxide – Indications enough showed you calls to make, horrors crawling inexorably towards goal in other flesh – What are you waiting for, kid? – slotless human wares? – nothing here now – Metamorphosis is complete – rings of Saturn in the dawn – The sky exploded question from vacant lots – youth nor age but as it were lips fading – There in our last filmountain street boy exploded 'the word', sits quietly silence to answer.

'You come with me, Meester to greet the garbage man and the dawn? traced fossil countenance everlastingly about the back door, Meester.' – dead post cards swept out by typewriters clatter hints as we shifted commissions – Hurry up please – crawling inexorably towards its goal – I – We – They – sit quietly in last terrace of the garden – The neon sun sinks in this sharp smell of carrion – (circling albatross – peeled noon – refuse like ash) – Ghost of Panama clung to our throats coughing and spitting in the fractured air, falling through space between worlds, we twisted slowly to black lagoons, flower floats and gondolas – tentative crystal city iridescent in the dawn wind – (Adolescents ejaculate over the tide flats) – Dead post card are you thinking of? – what thinking? – peeled noon and refuse like ash – Hurry up please – Make yourself a bit smart – Who is the third that walks beside you to a stalemate of black lagoons and violet light? last man – '

'You come with me, Meester?'

Up a great tidal river to the port city stuck in water hyacinths and banana rafts – The city is an intricate split bamboo structure in some places six storeys high overhanging the street propped up by beams and sections of railroad track and concrete pillars, an arcade from the warm rain that falls at half hour intervals – The coast people drift in the warm steamy night eating colored ices under the arc lights and converse in slow catatonic gestures punctuated by immobile silence – Plaintive boy cries drift through Night Of The Vagrant Ball Players

'Paco! – Joselito! – Henrique! – '

'A ver Luckees!'

'Where you go, Meester?'

'Squeezed down heads?'

Soiled mouth above a tuxedo blows smoke rings into the night 'SMOKE TRAK CIGARETTES. THEY LIKE YOU. TRAK LIKE ANY YOU. ANY TRAK LIKE YOU. SMOKE TRAKS. THEY SERVICE. TRAK TRAK TRAK.'

Leaping back kicking los Vagos Jugadores de Pelota storm the stale streets of commerce – Civil Guards discreetly turn away and open their fly to look for crabs in a vacant lot – For the Vagrant Ball Players can sound a Hey Rube Switch brings a million adolescents shattering the customs barriers and frontiers of time, swinging out of the jungle with Tarzan cries, crash landing perilous tin planes and rockets, leaping from trucks and banana rafts, charge through the black dust of mountain wind like death in the throat.

Native take refuge from guards in the vagrant night eating colored ices . . . Hey Rube switch brings a slow catatonic gesture . . .

Plaintive boy of the vagrant ball players: 'Planes and rockets?'

'A ver Luckees?'

'Nice girl Meester?'

'Squeak rubble of mountain wind?'

'Stale patter of commerce?'

The vagrant players back kick from June subway . . . drift through the night crash landing perilous animals . . .

'Kiki!'

'Paco!'

'Joselito!'

color comics in a blue wind . . . stale streets of officer wearing on in the mouth . . . Native, take it to Cut City . . . Orange light spoke out hour intervals in a vacant lot . . . Catatonic limestone liberates the area . . . This war will be won in color switch . . . The Trak sign stirs like a nocturnal beast and bursts into blue flame.

'SMOKE TRAK CIGARETTES. THEY LIKE YOU, TRAK LIKE ANY YOU. ANY TRAK LIKE YOU. SMOKE TRAKS. THEY SATISFY. THEY SERVICE. TRAK TRAK TRAK.'

'Vagos Jugadores de Pelota, sola esperanza del mundo, take it to Cut City – Street gangs Uranian born in the face of nova conditions, cut word lines, cut time lines – Take it to Cut City. muchachos – "minutes to go" – '

Jungle invades the weed grown parks where armadillos infected with the earth eating disease gambol through deserted kiosks and Bolivar in catatonic limestone liberates the area – Candiru infiltrate causeways and swimming pools – Albinos blink in the sun – A line of boys sitting under the arcades read color comics and masturbate to

Mambo . . . move legs . . . Car walks through . . . arcades Carl walks through overhanging stale streets of Railroad King . . . taste of iron in the mouth from June subways . . .

cities of wooden lattice and balconies flaking silver paint under grey metal fallout like cold melted solder on the streets and tenements of the terminal city where muttering cripples with phosporescent metal stumps drag through slow time streets eating brown metal meal in rusty troughs under orange gas flares . . . rank smell of rotten rivers and mud flats – swamp delta to the sky that does not change – islands of garbage where green boys with delicate purple gills tend chemical gardens – terminal post card shrinking in heavy time. muttering addicts of the orgasm drug. boneless in the sun, eaten alive by crab men – terminal post card shrinking in heavy time. 'Thing Police keep all Board Room Reports – Do not forget this Senor – '

They were searching his room when he returned from the Ministry Of Tourist Travel – fingers light and cold as Spring wind rustling papers and documents – One flashed a badge like a fish side in dark water –

'Police, Johnny.'

'Campers,' obviously – 'Campers' move into any government office and start issuing directives and spinning webs of inter office memos – Some have connections in high sources that will make the operation legal and exempt narcotic – Others are shoe string operators out of broom closets and dark rooms of the Mugging Department – They charge out high on ammonia issuing insane orders and requisitioning any object in their path – Tenuous bureaus spring up like sandstorms – The whole rancid oil scandal drifted out in growth areas –

Bradly was reading the sign nailed to a split bamboo tenement – The sign was printed on white paper book page size

> Cut The Sex And Dream Utility Lines//
> Cut The Trak Service Lines//
> The paws do not refresh//
> Clom Fliday Meester Surplus Oil//
> Working for the Yankee dollar?//
> Trak your own utilities//

Under silent wings of malaria a tap on his shoulder: 'Documentes, señor. Passaport.'

His passport drew them like sugar flashing gold teeth in little snarls of incredulity: 'Passaport no bueno! No en ordenes!'

The fuzz that could not penetrate to the passport began chanting in

unison: 'Comisaria! Comisaria! Comisaria! Meester a la Comisaria! –
Passaport muy malo. No good. No bueno. Typical sights leak out.'
The Commandante wore a green uniform spattered with oil and gave
out iron smoke as he moved – A small automatic moved round his
waist on metal tracks trailing blue sparks – Seedy agents click into
place with reports and documents.

'It is permiso, si to read the public signs. This' – His hand covered
the white sign on a split bamboo wall – 'is a special case.'

A man with a green eye shade slid forwards: 'Yes. That's what
they call it: "making a case" – It's all there in the files, the whole
rancid oil scandal of the Trak Sex And Dream Utilities in Growth
Areas.'

He pointed to a row of filing cabinets and lockers – Smell of
mouldy jock straps and chlorine drifted through the police terminal.
The Commandante turned the newspaper man back with a thin
brown hand: 'Much politics that one – It is better to be just technical.'

A swede Con Man hiding out in Rio Bamba under the cold souvenir of Chimborazi, junk cover removed for the non-payment, syndi-
cates of the world feeling for him with distant fingers of murder,
perfected that art along the Tang Dynasty in the back room of a
Chinese laundry. the Swede had one thing left: the grey felt hat
concession for 'Growth Areas' hidden under front companies and
aliases. With a 1910 magic lantern he posed Indians in grey felt hats
and broke the image into a million pieces reflected in dark eyes and
blue mountain ice and black water and piss and lamp chimneys,
tinted burocrat glasses, gun barrels, store fronts and cafe mirrors –
He flickered the broken image into the eyes of a shrunken head that
died in agony looking at a grey felt hat. And the head radiated: *Hat
... Hat ... Hat ... Hat ... Hat ...*

'It is a jumping head,' he said.

When the hat lines formed one thing that could break them was
orgasm – So he captured a missionary's wife and flickered her with
pornographic slides – And he took her head to radiate anti-sex – He
took other anti-sex heads in copraphillic vice and electric disgust –
He dimmed the sex and dream utilities of the land. And he was
shipped back to Sweden in a lead cylinder to found the Trak Service
and the Trak Board.

Trak has come a long way from a magic lantern in the Chink
laundry. The heads were donated to the Gothenberg Museum where
the comparatively innocuous emanations precipitated a mass sex
orgy.

Vagos Jugadores, sola esperanza del mundo, take it to Cut City. vista of red stone buildings and copper pagodas open air restaurants pools gardens and canals gold fish three feet long and giant pink salamanders . . . The black obsidian pyramid of Trak Home Office.

'The perfect product, gentlemen, has precise molecular affinity for its client of predilection. Someone urges the manufacture and sale of products that wear out. This is not the way of competitive elimination. Our product never leaves the customer. We sell the servicing and all Trak products have precise need of Trak servicing . . . The servicing of a competitor would act like antibiotics, offering to our noble Trak-strain services inedible counterpart . . . This is not just another habit-forming drug this is the habit-forming drug takes over all functions from the addict including his completely unnecessary under the uh circumstances and cumbersome skeleton. reducing him ultimately to the helpless condition of a larva. He may be said then to owe his very life such as it is to Trak servicing . . .'

The Trak Reservation so-called includes almost all areas in and about the United Republics of Freelandt and, since the Trak Police process all matters occurring in Trak Reservation and no one knows what is and is not Reservation, cases, civil and criminal are summarily removed from civilian courts with the single word *Trak* to unknown sanctions . . . Report meetings of Trak personnel are synchronized with other events as to a low pressure area . . . Benway was reporting so-called actually included almost the report meetings of Trak persona . . . Sometimes the Reservation is other persons and events in Trak guards sub type . . .

'Outskirts of Mexico City – Can't quite make it with all the guards around – Are you at all competent to teach me the language? Come in please with the images –'

'Trak police made us . . . Joe get going . . .'

So that is the whole story . . . a low pressure area . . . Circuit judge's sentence of death.

5

EARLY ANSWER

Corpses hang pants open on the road to Monterrey – clear and loud ahead naked post cards and baby shoes – A man comes back to something he left in underwear peeled the boy warm in 1929 – Thighs slapped the bed jumped ass up – 'Johnny screw' – Cup is split – wastings – Thermodynamics crawls home – game of empty hands – bed pictures post dead question – carrion smell sharp. open in

'Meester, jelly thing win you – Waiting for this?'

Streets of idiot pleasure – obsidian palaces of the fish city, bubbles twisting slow linen to the floor, traced fossils of orgasm

'You win something like jelly fish, Meester.'

His eyes calm and sad as little cats snapped the advantages: 'And I told him I said I am giving notice – Hanged in your dirty movies for the last time – Three thousand years in show business and I never stand still for such a routine like this.'

Street boys of the green with cruel idiot smiles and translucent amber flesh, aromatic jasmine excrement, pubic hairs that cut needles of pleasure – serving insect pleasures of the spine – alternate terminal flesh when the egg cracks.

'This bad place, Meester – This place of last fuck for Johnny.'

Smile of idiot death spasms – slow vegetable decay filmed his amber flesh – always there when the egg cracks and the white juice spurts from ruptured spines – from his mouth floated coal gas and violets – The boy dropped his rusty black pants – delicate musk of soiled linen – clothes stiff with oil on the red tile floor – naked and sullen his street boy senses darted around the room for scraps of advantage.

'You come with me Meester? Last flucky.'

Stranger color through his eyes the look out different, face transparent with all the sewers of death – hard ons spread nutty smells through the outhouse – soiled linen under the ceiling fan – spectral lust of shuttered rooms – He left a shirt on my bed

'Jimmy Sheffields is still as good as he used to be.'

'He was servicing customers shit, Meester – So Doctor Benway snapped the advantages – This special breed spitting notice: Egg

cracks the transmitter – Rat spines gathering mushroom flesh –
The boy dropped around your room for scraps – Got the rag on
body from vegetable – Dropped his pants and his cock.'

'Who are you? – My boat – .'

'Smells through the outhouse – A compost heap – Meester.'

Sacred Sewers of Death – boy dropped under the swamp
cypress flopping around in soiled linen – (started off on foot across
the deserted fields – A little hut on the outskirts – The writer
looked at both of us good as he used to be.) Idiot pictures started
coming in

'You win something like jelly with his knees up to the chin – sad
little irrigation ditch – Parrot on shoulder prods that heart –
Paralyzed, twisting in your movies for the last time – Out of me
from the waist down – I never stand still for such look out on
street boys of the green – Happened that boy could keep his gas
and violets – This spot advantages brown hands working in concert
for a switch to the drenched lands – Cyclatron shit these characters
– Come level on average smell under any image – evil odors high
around the other – Jimmy Sheffields is again as good – Street
boy's breath receiving notice – jelly routine like this – When the
egg cracks our spines servicing special customers of fossil orgasm.'

Kerosene lamp spattered light on red and white striped T shirt
and brown flesh – Dropped his pants – Pubic hairs cut stale
underwear fan whiffs of young hard on washing odors – afternoon
wind where the awning flaps

'Get physical with a routine like this? – Show you something
interesting: diseased flesh servicing frantic last fuck for Johnny –
film over the bed you know, eyes pop out – naked candy around
the room, scraps of adolescent image, hot semen in Panama –
Then the boy drops his drag and retires to a locker – *Who* look out
different? Who are *you* when their eyes pop out? – Mandrake
smells through the outhouse – The boy dropped and the boy
wakes up paralyzed – Remember there is only one visit: iron roof –
soiled linen under the clothes – scar tissue – shuttered room – evil
odors of food – I wasn't all that far from being good as I used to be
– Obsidian that broker before they get to him – A crab scuttles out
heavy – You win something like vacant lot – sad little patch right?
– boy face, green scarf – movies three up – You understand until I
die work I never stand still for. And such got the job – End getting
to know street boys of the green passport vending last fuck as his
pants drop.'

Dust of cities and wind faces came to world's end – call through remote dawn soaked in clouds, shivering back to mucous of the world.

Dust jissom in the bandana trailing afternoon wind – under black Stetson peeled his stale underwear – Kerosene lamp spattered light on .22, delicate legs and brown flesh – clothes stiff in the locker room rubbing each other – sullen as the other two watched – Stranger dropped his pants – Brown hands spurt it to the chest –

'Find time buyer – Start job – Image under the same position – Change place of your defense – '

'A Johannesberg beadonville he was servicing – Customers shitting Nigger for an eye cup of degenerates – Ejaculated the next day as Johnny – Meal mouthed cunt suckers flow through you – This special breed spitting cotton travel on a radar beam of service proof short bread – Shivering junk sick told your reporter the sex chucks hit us in heroin slow down – The paranoid ex Communist was there – Rubbed Moscow up me with a corkscrew motion of his limestones – Split is the wastings of the pool game – irritably for Mexico – By now we had floppy city in the distance, 1920s faint and intermittent – The track gave out forever an inch from the false bottom –

'They had torn down the transmitter – Rats was running the post – Somewhere North of Monterrey we meet in warring powers – Captured the spine clinic and cook down the prisoners for jelly – We are accused of soliciting with prehensile tree limbs – The first one dropped your defense his mouth bleeding – Got the rag on – Waiting to see this exhibit, dropped his pants and I came the spectroscope – You could smell it like a compost heap, pants just pulling in the winds of Panhandle – So we hit the Sacred Cotton Wood Grove – It's the only way to live – jissom under the swamp cypress – sweet shit of the street and the warm Spring wind to feel my cock – (dead bird in the black swamp water) – He would flop around in the trees, come five times in his dry goods.

'He told me he could fix back places – a little hut on the outskirts – pale blue sugary eyes that stuck to you – The writer looked at both of us and smiled a low pressure area, switch paper in his hands – weak and intermittent before the pictures started coming in: "Lawd Lawd have you seen my boy with his knees up to the chin pumping out spurts by the irrigation ditch?"

'When I shot my load I was paralyzed from the medicine – twisting in these spasms solid female siphoned out of me from the waist down – Shattering special type sex hangs from telegraph pole – And then I felt it way down in a carnival of splintered pink –

'Cold mountain shadows in the attic – and I went back with the boy to his cellar – Wonder whatever happened to that boy could keep a hard on all night? – A man comes back to something looking at the blue mountains – same thing day after day – world messages on the shit house wall – cock spurting limestone – summer dawn smell of boy balls so that was that – this spot where a lot of citizens will not work in concert – I didn't – Out for groceries and decided to whimper on the boys – We found Mother Green in your rubble along with some others from his deserted cock – Disgusting metamorphosis and a cyclatron shit these characters – (You wouldn't have a rope would you?) – Maybe I'm asking too many agriculturals –

'Come level on average we'll hold that old cow in line – Put any image in the soft drink would you? – Wet back asleep with a hard on was taken care of that way – Look, moving in whole armies and he sits me fishing lark – silent and shaking things considered and we moved out hard – around the other side piecing out the odds best we could – in the barn attic night and day smelling his thin cotton pants – He wakes buying it sight unseen.

'Jimmy busy doing *something* feller say – boys streaked with coal dust – Maybe I'm asking too many – (You wouldn't have a rope would you?) – Well now that bed room sitter boy his cock came up wet sleep – smiling looks at his crotch – peeled slow and touch it – springs out hard – Turns me around the end of his cock glistening – That smell through the dingy room clings to him like – Raw and peeled came to the hidden gallows – open door underneath to cut down ghost assassins – Odor of semen drifts in the brain – Jimmy with cruel idiot smile shacks elbows twisting him over on his candy – Found a pyjama cord and tied the boy – Jimmy lay there and suck his honey – Must have blacked out in the Mandrake Pub – So called Rock and Rollers crack wise on a lumpy studio bed with old shoes and overcoat some one cope – The boy wakes up paralyzed in hock – Sorted out name you never learned to use – Them marketable commodities turn you on direct connection come level on average – whiff of dried jissom in the price – I was on the roof so sweet young breath came through the time buyer –

'The gate in white flames – Early answer to the boy wakes naked – Down on his stomach is he? – Ah there and iron cool in the mouth – Come see me tonight in bone wrenching spasms –

Silver light pops something interesting – The boy features being younger of course – Wait a bit – No good at this rate – Try one if you want worthless old shit screaming without a body – Roll two years operation completed – We are? – Well the wind up is who? – Quien es? – World's end as a boy in drag retired to the locker – My page deals so many tasty ways on the bed – You know – Eyes pop out – candy and cigarettes what? – rectum open, the warm muscle boy rampant and spitting adolescent image – hot semen amok in Panama – scenic railways when their eyes pop out – Know the answer? – two ass holes and a mandrake – They'll do it every time – Rock and Rollers crack wise with overwhelming Minraud girl, wipe their ass on the women's toilet – and the boy wakes up paralyzed from arsenic and bleeding gums – Remember there is only one visit of a special kind – Flesh juice vampires is rotten smell of ice – No good no bueno outright or partially.

'Reason for the change of food he is subject to take back the keys – Square fact is that judges like it locked – Acting physician at Dankmoor fed up you understand until I die – End getting to know whose hanged man – One more chance still? – Come back to the Spanish bait, hard faced matron bandages the blotter – The shock when your neck breaks is far away – In this hotel room you are already dead of course – Boy stretches a leg, his cock flipped out – But uh well you see sputter of burning insect wings – '

In the sun at noon shirt open Kiki steps forward – With a wriggle stood naked spitting over the tide flats bare feet in dog's excrement – sad servant in sepia clouds of Panama

Predated checks bounce all around us in green place by the ball park – Come and jack off – passport vending machines – Jimmy walked along North End Road – (slow motion horses pulling carts – boy streaked with coal dust) – a low pressure area and the wind rising – Came to the World's End pissoir and met a boy with wide shoulders, black eyes glinting under the street lights, a heavy silk scarf tucked into his red and white striped T shirt – In the bedroom sitter the boy peeled off his clothes and sat down naked on the bed blowing cigarette smoke through his pubic hairs – His cock came up in the smoke – Switch blade eyes squinted, he watched with a smile wasn't exactly a smile as Jimmy folded his clothes – raw and peeled, naked now his cock pulsing – Jimmy picked up his key and put it in his mouth sucking the metal taste – The other sat smoking and silent – A slow drop of lubricant squeezed out the end of his cock glistening in light from the street

– Shutters clattered in the rising wind – A rotten vegetable smell seeped through the dingy room, shadow cars moved across the rose wall paper.

K9 had an appointment at the Sheffield Arms Pub but the short wave faded out on the location – Somewhere to the left? or was it to the right? – On? off? North End Road? – He walked through empty market booths, shutters clattering – Wind tore the cover off faces he passed raw and peeled – Came to World's End wind blowing through empty time pockets – No Sheffield Arms – Back to his room full of shadows – There he was sitting on the bed with the smile that wasn't exactly a smile – At the washbasin a boy was using his toothbrush –

'Who are these people?'

The boy turned from the washbasin 'You don't remember me? – Well we met in a way that is' – The toothbrush in his hand was streaked with blood.

Jimmy sat down on the bed his rectum tingling – The other picked up his scarf from a chair and ran it through his fingers looking at Jimmy with a cruel idiot smile – His hands closed on Jimmy's elbows twisting him over on his stomach down on the bed – The boy found a pyjama cord and tied Jimmy's hands behind his back – Jimmy lay there gasping and sucked the key, tasting metal in his mouth – The other straddled Jimmy's body – He spit on his hands and rubbed the spit on his cock – He placed his hands on Jimmy's ass cheeks and shoved them apart and dropped a gob of spit on the rectum – He slid the scarf under jimmy's hips and pulled his body up onto his cock – Jimmy gasped and moved with it – The boy slid the scarf up along jimmy's body to the neck –

He must have blacked out though he hadn't had much to drink at the pub – two so-called double brandies and two Barley wines – He was lying on a lumpy studio bed in a strange room – familiar too – in shoes and overcoat – someone else's overcoat – such a coat he would never have owned himself – a tweedy loose-fitting powder blue coat – K9 ran to tight-fitting black Chesterfields which he usually bought second hand in hock shops – He had very little money for clothes though he liked to dress in 'banker drag' he called it – black suits – expensive ties and linen shirts – Here he was in such a coat as he would never voluntarily have owned or worn – someone else's room – bed sitter – cheap furniture suitcases open – K9 found two keys covered with dust on the mantle – sat down convenient and sorted out his name – on the bed wasn't exactly a smile

'You never learned to use your Jimmy – slow with the right – there will be others behind him with the scarf – We met you know in a way that is in the smell of wine – You don't remember me?'

Taste of blood in his throat familiar too – and overcoat – someone else's – streaked with coal dust – The bed sitter boy as it always does folded his clothes – lay there gasping fresh in today

'Went into what might be called the comfortable and got myself a flat jewelry lying about wholesale side – Learned how to value them marketable commodities come level on average – Well groceries – She started screaming for a respectable price – I was on the roof so I had to belt her – Find a time buyer before doing sessions – There's no choice if they start job for instance – Have to let it go cheap and start further scream along the line – one or two reliable thieves – Work was steady at the gate to meet me – early answer to use on anyone considering to interfere – Once in a while I had to put it about but usually what you might call a journeyman thief – It was done so modern and convenient – Sorted out punishment and reward lark – On, off? The bed down on his stomach is he? Ah there you are behind him with the scarf – Hands from 1910 – There's no choice if took off his clothes – Have to let it go cheap and start naked.'

Twisted the scarf tighter and tighter around Jimmy's neck – Jimmy gasped coughing and spitting, face swollen with blood – His spine tingled – Coarse black hair suddenly sprouted all over him. Canines tore through his gums with exquisite toothache pain – He kicked in bone wrenching spasms. Silver light popped in his eyes.

He decided to take the coat with him – Might pass someone on the stairs and they would think he was the tenant since the boy resembled him in build and features being younger of course but then people are not observant come level on average – Careful –

'Careful – watch the exits – Wait a bit – No good at this rate – Watch the waves and long counts – No use moving out – Try one if you want to – All dies in convulsions screaming without a body – Know the answer? – Arsenic two years: operation completed – WE are arsenic and bleeding gums – Who? Quien es? – World's End loud and clear – So conjured up wide shoulders and black eyes glinting – shadow cars through the dingy room – My page deals the bedroom sitter out of suitcase here on the bed where you know me with cruel idiot smile as Jimmy's eyes pop out – Silk scarf moved up rubbing – Pubic hair sprouted all over him tearing the flesh like wire – Eyes squinted from a smell I always feel – Hot spit burned his rectum open – The warm muscle contracts – Kicked breathless coughing and spitting adolescent image blurred in film smoke – through the gums the fist in his face – taste of blood – His broken body spurted life in other flesh – identical erections in the kerosene lamp – electric hair sprouted in ass and genitals – taste of blood in the throat – hot semen spurted idiot mambo – one boy naked in Panama – Who? – Quien es? – Compost heap stench where you know me from – a smell I always feel when his eyes pop out – '

'Know the answer? Arsenic two years: goof ball bum in 1910 Panama. They'll do it every time – Vampires is no good all possessed by overwhelming Minraud girl – '

'Are you sure they are not for protection?'

'Quite sure – Nothing here but to borrow your body for a special purpose: ("Excellent – Proceed to the ice.") – in the blood arsenic and bleeding gums – They were addicted to this round of whatever visits of a special kind – An errand boy of such a taste took off his clothes – indications enough naked now his cock healed scar tissue – Flesh juice vampires is no good – all sewage – sweet rotten smell of ice – no use of them better than they are – The whole thing tell you no good no bueno outright or partially.'

'Reasons for the change of food not wholly disinterested – The square fact is that judges like a chair – For many years he used Parker – Fed up with present food in the Homicide Act and others got the job – So think before time that abolition is coming anyway after that, all the top jobbies would like to strike a bargain in return for accepting the end of hanging – Generous? Nothing – I wasn't all that far from being in position – '

'Have to move fast – Nail that broker before they get to him – Doing him a favor any case – '

He found the Broker in a cafe off the Socco – heavy with massive muscled flesh and cropped grey hair – K9 stood in the shadow and tugged his mind screen – the Broker stood up and walked down an alley – K9 stepped out of the shadows in his new overcoat –

'Oh it's you – Everything all right? – '

K9 took off his hat respectfully and covered his gun with it – He had stuffed the hat with the Green Boy's heavy silk scarf – a crude silencer but there was nobody in the alley – It wasn't healthy to be within earshot when the Broker had business with anyone – He stood with the hat an inch from the Broker's mid section – He looked into the cold grey eyes –

'Everything is just fine' he said –

And pumped three Police Specials into the massive stomach hard as a Japanese wrestler – The Broker's mouth flew open sucking for breath that did not come – K9 gave him three more and stepped aside – The Broker folded, slid along a wall and flopped face up his eyes glazing over – Lee dropped the burning hat and scarf on a pile of excrement and walked out of the alley powder smoke drifting from his cheap European suit – He walked toward flesh of Spain and Picadilly –

'Wind hand to the hilt – fed up you understand until I die – work we have to do and way got the job – end getting to know whose reports are now ended – "One more change" he said "touching circumstance". – Have you still – Come back to the Spanish bait it's curtains under his blotter'

Who? Quien es? – Question is far away – In this hotel room you are writing whiffs of Spain – Boy stretches a leg – His cock flipped out in the kerosene lamp – sputter of burning insect wings – heard the sea – tin shack over the mud flats – erogenous holes and pepper smells –

In the sun at noon shirt open as his pants dropped – lay on his stomach and produced a piece of soap rubbed the soap in – He gasped and moved with it – whiffs of his feet in the warm Summer afternoon –

Who? Quien es? – It can only be the end of the world ahead loud and clear –

Kiki steps forward on faded photo – Pants slipping down legs with a wriggle stood naked spitting on his hands – Shot a bucket grinning – over the whispering tide flats youths in the act, pants down, bare feet in dog's excrement – Street smells of the world siphoned back red and white T shirt to brown Johnny – that stale dawn smell of naked sleep under the ceiling fan – Shoved him over on his stomach kicking with slow pleasure –

'Hooded dead gibber in the turnstile – What used to be me is backward sound track – fossil orgasm kneeling to inane cooperation.' wind through the pissoir – 'J'aime ces types vicieux qu'ici montrent la bite' – green place by the water pipe – dead leaves caught in pubic hairs – 'Come and jack off – 1929' – Woke in stale smell of vending machines – The boy with grey flannel pants stood there grinning a few inches in his hand – shadow cars and wind through other flesh – came to World's End. brief boy on screen revolving lips and pants and forgotten hands in countries of the world –

On the sea wall met a boy in red and white T shirt under a circling albatross – 'Brown Meester?' – warm rain on the iron roof – The boy peeled his stale underwear – Identical erection flipped out in kerosene lamp – The boy jumped on the bed, slapped his thighs: 'I screw Johnny up ass? Asi como perros' – Rectums merging to idiot Mambo – One boy naked in Panama dawn wind –

In the hyacinths the green boys smile – rotting music trailing vines and bird calls through remote dreamy lands – The initiate awoke in that stale summer dawn smell, suitcases all open on a brass bed in Mexico – mucous of the world – in the shower a Mexican about twenty, rectums naked, smell of carbolic soap and barrack toilets –

Trails my summer dawn wind in other flesh strung together on scar impressions of young Panama night – open shirt flapping in the pissoir – Cock flipped out and up – water from his face – the boy's slender tight ass

'Breathe in, Johnny – Here goes – '

They was ripe for the plucking forgot way back yonder in the corn hole – lost in little scraps of delight and burning scrolls – through the open window trailing swamp smells and old newspapers – rectums naked in whiffs of raw meat – genital smells of the two bodies merge in shared meals and belches of institution cooking – spectral smell of empty condoms down along penny arcades and mirrors – Forgotten shadow actor walks beside you – mountain wind of Saturn in the morning sky – From the death trauma weary goodbye then – orgasm addicts stacked in the attic like muttering burlap –

Odor rockets over oily lagoons – Silver flakes fall through a maze of dirty pictures – windy city outskirts – smell of empty condoms, excrement, black dust – ragged pants to the ankle –

Bone faces – neetles along adobe walls open shirts flapping – savannah and grass mud – The sun went – The mountain shadow touched ragged pants – whisper of dark street in faded Panama photo – 'Muy got good one, Meester' smiles through the pissoir – Orgasm siphoned back street smells and a Mexican boy – Woke in the filtered green light, thistle shadows cutting stale underwear –

The three boys lay on the bank rubbing their stomachs against the warm sand – They stood up undressing to swim – They swam lazily letting the warm water move between their legs and Lloyd walked back to his pants and brought a piece of soap and they passed it back and forth laughing and rubbing each other and Billy ejaculated his thin brown stomach arched out of the water as the spurts shot up in the sunlight like tiny rockets – He sagged down into the water panting and lay there against the muddy bottom – breathing sewage smells of the canal.

Under the old tressil trailing vines in the warm Summer afternoon undressing to swim and rubbing their bellies – Lloyd rubbing his hand down further and further openly rubbing his crotch now and grinning as the other two watched and Billy looked at Jimmy hesitantly and began to rub too and slowly Jimmy did the same – They came into the water watching the white blobs drift away –

Stale underwear of penny arcades slipping down legs, rectums feeling the warm sun, laughing and washing each other soapy hands in his crotch, pearly spasms stirring the warm water –

The Mexican dropped his pants with a wriggle and stood naked in the filtered green light, vines on his back –

Ali squirmed teeth bared grinning – 'You is coming, Johnny?' – sunlight on the army blankets – orgasm crackled with electric afternoon – bodies stuck together in magnetic eddies –

Shoved him over on his stomach kicking – The Mexican held his knees – Hand dipped a piece of soap – Shoved his cock in laughing – bodies stuck together in the sunlight kicked whiffs of rectal mucous – laughing teeth and pepper smells –

'You is feeling the hot quick Mexican kid naked Mambo to your toes Johnny . . . dust in bare leg hairs tight brown nuts preech very hot . . . How long you want us to fuck very nice Meester? Flesh diseased dirty pictures we fucking tired of fuck very nice Mister.' Sad image of sickness at the attic window say something to you "*adios*" worn out film washed back in prep school clothes to distant closing dormitory fragments off the page stained toilet pictures blurred rotting pieces of "Freckle Leg" dormitory dawn dripping water on his face diseased voice so painful telling you "Sparks" is over New York. Have I done the job here? With a telescope you can watch our worn out film dim jerky far away shut a bureau drawer faded sepia smile from an old calendar falling leaves sun cold on a thin boy with freckles folded away in an old file now standing last review – times lost or strayed long empty cemetery with a mouldy pawn ticket – fading whisper down skid row to Market Street shows all kinds masturbation and self-abuse – Young boys need it special'

silver paper in the wind distant 1920 wind and dust. He was looking at some thing a long time ago where the second hand book shop used to be just opposite the old cemetery

'Dead young flesh in stale underwear vending sex words to magnetic Law 334 – Indicates simple tape is served sir, through iron repetition – Ass and genitals tingling in 1929 jack off spelt out broken wings of Icarus – Control system ousted from half the body whispers skin instructions to memory of melting ice – area of Spain – channels ahead loud and clear – Line of the body fitted to other underwear and Kiki steps forward on faded photo – sad image dusted by the Panama night –

'So think before they can do any locks over the Chinese that abolition is war of the past – The end of hanging generous? Just the same position – Changed place of years in the end is just the same –

call through remote dawn of back yards and ash pits – plaintive ghost in the turnstile – Shadow cars and wind faces came to World's End – whiff of dried jissom in the bandana trailing sweet young breath through remote lands – soft globs on a brass bed in Mexico – naked – wet – carbolic soap – tight nuts – piece of soap in the locker room rubbing each other off to "My Blue Heaven" – grinning as the other two watched – Summer dawn smell of his crotch –

'Changed place? – Same position – Sad image circulates through backward time – Clom Fliday.'

He came Friday. We got to untalking on question studying the porch noise home from work . . .

'Used to be me Mister.'

diseased waiting face dim jerky far away dawn in his eyes 'Are you tracking me? Know who I am?'

So I hit Miami airport a tick ahead of the geigers . . .

'Are your roast beef sandwiches hot?'

'All our sandwiches are cold.'

She said it heavy and cold as a cop's blackjack on a winter night and laid out a sandwich on the counter soaked through with cold wet lettuce.

'Are you tracking me? Know who I am? I am a survivor of Flight 52.'

I walk out into the airport and see something interesting. It is a whole school of idiots – 'retarded children' if you are the type person calls a cracker a southern gentleman – all holding hands for protection with cards around their necks this package is destined for a special shoot in Connecticut. I nip into the Gentlemen locate a remote booth and slip a plastic bag of U.T. – Undifferentiated Tissue – out of my brief case which being uncured Mexican stinks like a dead 'gator which is nothing to the stink this U.T. gives out with when I break the seal and mould myself a handsome lowering idiot face and powerful torso. That U.T. burns like napalm and I black out from the pain. Then I am back with a hot hard on. Wait till lights out in the old dorm tonight. I walk out smelling like an accident the way an idiot will and grabs myself a retarded hand. Some old doll is sniffing and looking so I rounds on her and says

'I know you lady? Who you trying to hypnotise?'

She come near to have an accident herself. I sit down and wallow in my U.T. like an alligator rubbing my crotch slow when some square gives me the eye and he look away again fast I can tell you. Have to move fast. That U.T. only last 72 hours

'Are you tracking me? Know who I am?'

The name is Clem Snide – I am a Private Ass Hole – I will take on any job any identity any body – I will do anything difficult dangerous or downright dirty for a price –

The man opposite me didn't look like much – a thin grey man in a long coat that flickered like old film – He just happens to be the biggest operator in any time universe –

'I don't care myself you understand' – He watched the ash spiralling down from the end of his Havana – It hit the floor in a puff of grey dust –

'Just like that – Just time – Just time – Don't care myself if the whole fucking shit house goes up in chunks – I've sat out novas before – I was born in a nova.'

'Well Mr. Martin, I guess that's what birth is you might say.'

'I wouldn't say – Have to be moving along any case – The ticket that exploded posed little time – Point is they are trying to cross me up – small timers – still on the old evacuation plan – Know what the old evacuation plan is, Mr. Snide?'

'Not in detail.'

'The hanging gimmick – death in orgasm – gills – no bones and elementary nervous system – evacuation to The Drench Lands – a bad deal on the level and it's not on the level with Sammy sitting in – small timers trying to cross me up – Me, Bradly-Martin, who invented the double cross – '

6

CASE OF THE CELLULOID KALI

'Step right up – Now you see me now you don't – A few scores to settle before I travel – A few things to tidy up and that's where you come in – I want you to contact the Venus Mob, the Vegetable People and spill the whole fucking compost heap through Times Square and Piccadilly – I'm not taking any rap for that green bitch – I'm going to rat on everybody and split this dead whistle stop planet wide open – I'm clean for once with the nova heat – like clean fall out – '

He faded in spiralling patterns of cigar smoke – There was a knock at the door registered letter from Antwerp – ten thousand dollar check for film rights to a novel I hadn't written called *The Soft Ticket* – letter from somebody I never heard of who is acting as my agent suggests I contact the Copenhagen office to discuss the Danish rights on my novel *Expense Account* –

Bar backed by pink shell – New Orleans jazz thin in the Northern night. A boy slid off a white silk bar stool and held out the hand: 'Hello, I'm Johnny Yen, a friend of – Well, just about everybody. I was more physical before my accident you can see from this interesting picture. Only the head was reduced to this jelly but like I say it the impression on my face was taken by the other man's eyes drive the car head-on it was and the Big Physician (he's very technical) rushed him off to a surgery and took out his eyes and made a quick impression and slapped it on me like a pancake before I started to dry out and curl around the edges. So now I'm back in harness you might say: thru the flesh and I have All of "*You*" that what I want from my audience is the last drop then bring me another. The place is hermetic. We think so blockade we thought nobody could get thru our flak thing. They thought. Switch Artist me. Oh, there goes my frequency. I'm on now ...'

The lights dimmed and Johnny pranced out in goggles flickering Northern Lights wearing a jockstrap of Undifferentiated Tissue that must be in constant movement to avoid crystallization. A penis rose out of the jock and dissolved in pink light back to a clitoris, balls retract into cunt with a fluid plop. Three times he did this to wild 'Holés!' from the audience. Drifted to the bar and ordered a heavy blue drink. D noted patches of white crystal formed along the scar lines on Johnny's copy face.

'Just like canals. Maybe I'm a Martian when the crystals are down.'

You will die there a screwdriver through the head. The thought like looking at me over steak and explain it all like that stay right here. She was also a Reichian Analyst. Disappear more or less remain in acceptable form to you the face.

'We could go on cutting my cleavage act, but genug basta assez dice fall hombre long switch street . . . I had this terrible accident in a car a Bentley it was I think they're so nice that's what you pay for when you buy one it's yours and you can be sure nobody will pull it out from under our assets. Of course we don't have assholes here you understand somebody might go and get physical. So we are strictly from urine. And that narrows things to a fine line down the middle fifty feefty and what could be fairer than that my Uncle Eyetooth always says he committed fornication but I don't believe it me old heavy water junky like him . . . So anyhoo to get back to my accident in my Bentley once I get my thing in a Bentley it's mine already.

'So we had this terrible accident or rather he did. Oh dear what am I saying? It wasn't my first accident you understand yearly wounded or was it monthly Oh dear I must stay on that middle line . . .

'Survivor. Survivor. Not the first in my childhood. Three thousand years in show business and always keep my nose clean. Why I was a dancing boy for the Cannibal Trog Women in the Ice Age. Remember? All that meat stacked up in the caves and the Blue Queen covered with limestone flesh creeps into your bones like cold grey honey . . . that's the way they keep them not dead but paralyzed with this awful stuff they cook down from vampire. bats get in your hair Gertie always keep your hair way up inside with a vampire on premises bad to get in other alien premises. The Spanish have this word for it, something about props ajeno or something like that I know so am ya la yo mixa everything allup. They call me Puto The Cement Mixer, now isn't that cute? Some people think I'm just silly but I'm not silly at all . . . and this boyfriend told me I looked just like a shrew with my ears quivering hot and eager like burning leaves and those were his last words engraved on my back tape – along with a lot of other old memories that disgust me, you wouldn't believe the horrible routines I been involved through my profession of Survival Artist ... and they think that's funny, but I don't laugh except real quick between words no time you understand laughing they could get at me doesn't keep them off like talking does, now watch – '

A flicker pause and the light shrank and the audience sound a vast muttering in Johnny's voice.

'You see' – Shadows moved back into nightclub seats and drank nightclub drinks and talked nightclub talk – 'They'd just best is all. So I was this dancing boy for these dangerous old cunts paralyzed men and boys they dug special stacked right up to the ceiling like the pictures I saw of Belsen or one of those awful contracted places and I said they are at it again ... I said the Old Army Game. I said "Pass The Buck". Now you see it, now you don't ... Paralyzed with this awful gook the Sapphire Goddess let out through this cold sore she always kept open on her lips, that is a hole in the limestone you understand she was like entirely covered with one of those stag rites ... Real concentrated in there and irradiated to prevent an accident owing to some virus come lately wander in from Podunk Hepatitis ... But I guess I'm talking too much about private things ... But I know this big atomic professor, he's very technical too, says: "There are no secrets any more, Pet" when I was smooching around him for a quickie. My Uncle still gives me a sawski for a hot nuclear secret and ten years isn't hay, dahling, in these times when practically anybody is subject to wander in from the desert with a quit claim deed and snatch a girl's snatch right out from under her assets ... over really I should say but some of we boys are so sick we got this awful cunt instead of a decent human asshole disgust you to see it ... So I just say anything I hear on the old party line.

'I used to keep those old cave cunts at bay with my Impersonation Number where I play this American Mate Dance in Black Widow drag and I could make my face flap around you wouldn't believe it and the noises I made in uh orgasm when She ate me – I played both parts you unnerstand, imitated The Goddess Herself and turn right into stone for security ... And She couldn't give me enough juice running out of this hole was her only orifice and she was transported dais and all, die ass and all, by blind uniques with no balls, had to crawl under Her dais dressed in Centipede Suit Of The Bearer which was put on them as a great honor and they was always fighting over matters of protocrawl ... So all these

boys stacked to the ceiling covered with limestone ... you understand they weren't dead any more than a fresh oyster is dead, but
died in the moment when the shell was cracked and they were
eaten all quivering sweet and tasty. vitamins the right way ...
eaten with little jewelled adzes jade and sapphires and chicken
blood rubies all really magnificent. Of course I pinched everything
I could latch onto with my prehensile piles I learned it boosting in
Chi to pay the luxury tax on C. three thousand years in show
business ... later or was it earlier, the Mayan Calendar is all
loused up you know ... I was a star Corn God inna Sacred
Hanging Ceremony to fructify the corn devised by this impresario
who specializes in these far out bit parts which fit me like a
condom, he says the cutest things. He's a doctor too, a Big
Physician made my face over after "The Accident" collided with
my Bentley head on ... the cops say they never see anything so
intense and it is a special pass I must be carrying I wasn't
completely obliterated.

'Oh there's my doctor made the face over after my accident. He
calls me Pygmalion now, isn't that cute? You'll love him.'

The doctor was sitting in a surgical chair of gleaming nickel. His
soft boneless head was covered with grey green fuzz, the right side
of his face an inch lower than the left side swollen smooth as a boil
around a dead, cold undersea eye.

'Doctor, I want you to meet my friend Mister D The Agent, and
he's a lovely fellow too.

('Some time he don't hardly hear what you saying. He's very
technical.')

The doctor reached out his abbreviated fibrous fingers in which
surgical instruments caught neon and cut Johnny's face into
fragments of light.

'Jelly,' the Doctor said, liquid gurgles through his hardened
purple gums. His tongue was split and the two sections curled over
each other as he talked: 'Life jelly. It sticks and grows on you like
Johnny.'

Little papules of tissue were embedded in the doctor's hands.
The doctor pulled a scalpel out of Johnny's ear and trimmed the
papules into an ash tray where they stirred slowly exuding a green
juice.

'They say his prick didn't synchronize at all so he cut it off and
made some kinda awful cunt between the two sides of him He got
a whole ward full of his "fans" he call them already.

'When the wind is right you can hear them scream in Town Hall Square. And everybody says "But this is interesting."

'I was more *physical* before my *accident*, you can see from this interesting picture.'

Lee looked from the picture to the face, saw the flickering phosphorescent scars –

'Yes' he said 'I know you – You're dead nada walking around visible.'

So the boy is rebuilt and gives me the eye and there he is again walking around some day later across the street and 'No dice' flickered across his face – The copy there is a different being, something ready to slip in – boys empty and banal as sunlight her way always – So he is exact replica is he not? – empty space of the original –

So I tailed the double to London on the Hook Von Holland and caught him out strangling a naked faggot in the bed sitter – I slip on the antibiotic hand cuffs and we adjourn to the Mandrake Club for an informative little chat –

'What do you get out of this?' I ask bluntly.

'A smell I always feel when their eyes pop out' – The boy looked at me his mouth a little open showing the whitest teeth this Private Eye ever saw – naval uniform buttoned in the wrong holes quilted with sea mist and powder smoke, smell of chlorine, rum and mouldy jock straps – And probably a narcotics agent is hiding in the spare stateroom that is always locked – There are the stairs to the attic room he looked out of and his mother moving around – dead she was they say – dead – with such hair too – red.

'Where do you feel it?' I prodded.

'All over' he said, eyes empty and banal as sunlight – 'Like hair sprouting all over me' – He squirmed and giggled and creamed in his dry goods –

'And after every job I get to see the movies – You know – And he gave me the sign twisting his head to the left and up –

So I gave him the sign back and the words jumped in my throat all there like and ready the way they always do when I'm right 'You make the pilgrimage?'

'Yes – The road to Rome.'

I withdrew the antibiotics and left him there with that dreamy little boy look twisting the napkin into a hangman's knot – On the bus from the air terminal a thin grey man sat down beside me – I offered him a cigarette and he said 'Have one of mine' and I see he is throwing the tin on me – 'Nova police – You are Mr Snide I believe' And he moved right in and shook me down looking at pictures, reading letters checking back on my time track

'There's one of them' I heard some one say as he looked at a photo in my files.

'Hummm – yes – and here's another – Thank you Mr Snide – You have been most cooperative – '

I stopped off in Bologna to look up my old friend Green Tony thinking he could probably give me a line – up four flights in a tenement past the old bitch selling black market cigarettes and cocaine cut with Saniflush, through a dirty brown curtain and there is Green Tony in a pad with Chinese jade all over and Etruscan cuspidors – He is sitting back with his leg thrown over an Egyptian throne smoking a cigarette in a carved emerald holder – He doesn't get up but he says: 'Dick Tracy in the flesh' and motions to a Babylonian couch.

I told him what I was after and his face went a bright green with rage 'That stupid bitch – She bringa the heat on all of us – *Nova heat* – ' He blew a cloud of smoke and it hung there solid in front of him – Then he wrote an address in the smoke – 'No 88 Via di Nile, Roma'

This 88 Nile turned out to be one of those bar-soda fountains like they have in Rome – You are subject to find a maraschino cherry in your dry martini and right next to some citizen is sucking a banana split disgust you to see it – Well I am sitting there trying not to see it so I look down at the far end of the counter and dug a boy very dark with kinky hair and something Abyssinian in his face – Our eyes lock and I give him the sign – And he gives it right back – So I spit the maraschino cherry in the bartender's face and slip him a big tip and he says 'Rivideci and bigger'.

And I say 'Up yours with a double strawberry phosphate'.

The boy finishes his pink lady and follows me out and I take him back to my trap and right away get into an argument with the clerk about no visitors extranjeri to the hotel – enough garlic on his breath to deter a covey of vampires – I shove a handful of lires into his mouth 'Go buy yourself some more gold teeth' I told him –

When this boy peeled off the dry goods he gives off a slow stink like a thawing mummy – But his ass hole sucked me right in all my experience as a Private Eye never felt anything like it – In the flash bulb of orgasm I see that fucking clerk has stuck his head through the transom for a refill – Well expense account – The boy is lying there on the bed spreading out like a jelly slow tremors running through it and sighs and says: 'Almost like the real thing isn't it?'

And I said 'I need the time milking' and give him the sign so heavy come near slipping a disk.

'I can see you're one of our own' he said warmly sucking himself back into shape – 'Dinner at eight' – He comes back at eight in a souped up Ragazzi and we take off 160 per and scream to stop in front of a villa I can see the Benzleys and Hispano Bear Cats and Studz Suisses and what not piled up and all the golden youth of Europe is disembarking – 'Leave your clothes in the vestibule' the butler tells us and we walk in on a room full of people all naked to a turn sitting around on silk stools and a bar with a pink shell behind it – This cunt undulates forward and give me the sign and holds out her hand 'I am the Countessa di Vile your hostess for tonight' – She points to the boys at the bar with her cigarette holder and their cocks jumped up one after the other – And I did the polite thing too when my turn came –

So all the boys began chanting in unison '*The movies! – The movies! –* We want *the movies! –* ' So she led the way into the projection room which was filled with pink light seeping through the walls and floor and ceiling – The boy was explaining to me that these were actual films taken during the Abyssinian War and how lucky I was to be there – Then the action starts – There on the screen is a gallows and some young soldiers standing around with prisoners in loin cloths – the soldiers are dragging this kid up onto the gallows and he biting and screaming and shitting himself and his loin cloth slips off and they shove him under the noose and one of them tightens it around his neck standing there now mother naked – Then the trap fell and he drops kicking and yelping and you could hear his neck snap like a stick in a wet towel – He hangs there pulling his knees up to the chest and pumping out spurts of jissom and the audience coming right with him spurt for spurt – So the soldiers strip the loin cloths off the others and they all got hard ons waiting and watching – Got through a hundred of them more or less one at a time – Then they run the movie in slow motion slower and slower and you are coming slower and slower until it took an hour and then two hours and finally all the boys are standing there like statues getting their rocks off geologic – Meanwhile an angle comes dripping down and forms a stalagtite in my brain and I slip back to the projection room and speed up the movie so the hanged boys are coming like machine guns – Half the guests explode straightaway from altered pressure chunks of limestone whistling through the air. The others are flopping around on the floor like beeched idiots and the Countess gasps out 'Carbon dioxide for the love of Kali!' – So somebody turned on the carbon dioxide tanks and I made it out of there in an aqualung – Next thing the nova heat moves in and bust the whole aquarium.

'Humm, yes, and here's another planet – '

The officer moved back dissolving most cooperative connections formed by the parasite – Self righteous millions stabbed with rage.

'That bitch – She bringa the heat three dimensional.'

'The ugly cloud of smoke hung there solid female blighted continent – This turned out to be one of those association locks in Rome – I look down at the end – He quiets you, remember? – Finis. So I split the planet from all the pictures and give him a place of residence with inflexible authority – Well, no terms – A hand has been taken – Your name fading looks like – Madison Avenue machine disconnected.'

7

THE MAYAN CAPER

Joe Brundige brings you the shocking story of The Mayan Caper exclusive to The Evening News –

A Russian scientist has said: 'We will travel not only in space but in time as well' – I have just returned from a thousand year time trip and I am here to tell you what I saw – And to tell you how such time trips are made – It is a precise operation – It is difficult – It is dangerous – It is the new frontier and only the adventurous need apply – But it belongs to *anyone* who has the courage and know how to enter – it belongs to *you* –

I started my trip in the morgue with old newspapers, folding in today with yesterday and typing out composites – When you skip through a newspaper as most of us do you see a great deal more than you know – In fact you see it all on a subliminal level – Now when I fold today's paper in with yesterday's paper and arrange the pictures to form a time section montage, I am literally moving back to the time when I read yesterday's paper, that is traveling in time back to yesterday – I did this eight hours a day for three months – I went back as far as the papers went – I dug out old magazines and forgotten novels and letters – I made fold-ins and composites and I did the same with photos –

The next step was carried out in a film studio – I learned to talk and think backwards on all levels – This was done by running film and sound track backwards – For example a picture of myself eating a full meal was reversed, from satiety back to hunger – First the film was run at normal speed, then in slow motion – The same procedure was extended to other physiological processes including orgasm – (It was explained to me that I must put aside all sexual prudery and reticence, that sex was perhaps the heaviest anchor holding one in present time.) For three months I worked with the studio – My basic training in time travel was completed and I was now ready to train specifically for the Mayan assignment –

I went to Mexico City and studied the Mayans with a team of archaeologists – The Mayans lived in what is now Yucatan, British Honduras, and Guatemala – I will not recapitulate what is known of their history, but some observations on the Mayan calendar are essential to understanding this report – The Mayan calendar starts from a mythical date 5 Ahua 8 Cumhu and rolls on to the end of the world also a definite date depicted in the codices as a God pouring water on the earth – The Mayans had a solar, a lunar, and a ceremonial calendar rolling along like interlocking wheels from 5 Ahua 8 Cumhu to the end – The absolute power of the priests, who formed about 2% of the population, depended on their control of this calendar – The extent of this number monopoly can be deduced from the fact that the Mayan verbal language contains no number above ten – Modern Mayan speaking Indians use Spanish numerals – Mayan agriculture was of the slash and burn type – ploughs can not be used in the Mayan area because there is a strata of limestone six inches beneath the surface and the slash and burn method is used to this day – Now slash and burn agriculture is a matter of precise timing – The brush must be cut at a certain time so it will have time to dry and the burning operation carried out before the rains start – A few days' miscalculation and the year's crop is lost –

The Mayan writings have not been fully deciphered, but we know that most of the hieroglyphs refer to dates in the calendar, and these numerals have been translated – It is probable that the other undeciphered symbols refer to the ceremonial calendar – There are only three Mayan codices in existence, one in Dresden, one in Paris, one in Madrid the others having been burned by Bishop Landa – Mayan is very much a living language and in the more remote villages nothing else is spoken – More routine work – I studied Mayan and listened to it on the tape recorder and mixed Mayan in with English – I made innumerable photo montages of Mayan codices and artifacts – the next step was to find a 'vessel' – We sifted through many candidates before settling on a young Mayan worker recently arrived from Yucatan – This boy was about twenty, almost black, with the sloping forehead and curved nose of the ancient Mayans – (The physical type has undergone little alteration) – He was illiterate – He had a history of epilepsy – He was what mediums call a 'sensitive' – For another three months I worked with the boy on the tape recorder mixing his speech with mine – (I was quite fluent in Mayan at this point – Unlike Aztec it is an easy language) It was time now for 'the transfer operation' – 'I' was to be moved into the body of this young Mayan – The operation is illegal and few are competent to practise it – I was referred to an American doctor who had become a heavy metal addict and lost his certificate – 'He is the best transfer artist in the industry' I was told 'For a price.'

We found the doctor in a dingy office on the Avenida Cinco de Mayo – He was a thin grey man who flickered in and out of focus like an old film – I told him what I wanted and he looked at me from a remote distance without warmth or hostility or any emotion I had ever experienced in myself or seen in another – He nodded silently and ordered the Mayan boy to strip, and ran practised fingers over his naked body – The doctor picked up a box like instrument with electrical attachments and moved it slowly up and down the boy's back from the base of the spine to the neck – The instrument clicked like a geiger counter – The doctor sat down and explained to me that the operation was usually performed with 'the hanging technique' – The patient's neck is broken and during the orgasm that results he passes into the other body – This method, however, was obsolete and dangerous – For the operation to succeed you must work with a pure vessel who has not been subject to parasite invasion – Such subjects are almost impossible to find in present time he stated flatly – His cold grey eyes flicked across the young Mayan's naked body:

'This subject is riddled with parasites – If I were to employ the barbarous method used by some of my learned colleagues – (nameless ass holes) – you would be eaten body and soul by crab parasites – My technique is quite different – I operate with moulds – Your body will remain here intact in deep freeze – On your return, if you do return, you can have it back' He looked pointedly at my stomach sagging from sedentary city life – 'You could do with a stomach tuck, young man – But one thing at a time – The transfer operation will take some weeks – And I warn you it will be expensive.'

I told him that cost was no object – The News was behind me all the way – He nodded briefly: 'Come back at this time tomorrow.' When we returned to the doctor's office he introduced me to a thin young man who had the doctor's cool removed grey eyes – 'This is my photographer – I will make my moulds from his negatives' The photographer told me his name was Jiminez – ('Just call me "Jimmy The Take"') – We followed 'The Take' to a studio in the same building equipped with a 35 Milometer movie camera and Mayan back drops – He posed us naked in erection and orgasm, cutting the images in together down the middle line of our bodies – Three times a week we went to the doctor's office

– He looked through rolls of film his eyes intense, cold, impersonal – And ran the clicking box up and down our spines – Then he injected a drug which he described as a variation of the apomorphine formulae – The injection caused simultaneous vomiting and orgasm and several times I found myself vomiting and ejaculating in the Mayan vessel – The doctor told me these exercises were only the preliminaries and that the actual operation, despite all precautions and skill, was still dangerous enough.

At the end of three weeks he indicated the time has come to operate – He arranged us side by side naked on the operating table under flood lights – With a phosphorescent pencil he traced the middle line of our bodies from the cleft under the nose down to the rectum – Then he injected a blue fluid of heavy cold silence as word dust fell from demagnetized patterns – From a remote Polar distance I could see the doctor separate the two halves of our bodies and fitting together a composite being – I came back in other flesh the look out different, thoughts and memories of the young Mayan drifting through my brain –

The doctor gave me a bottle of the vomiting drug which he explained was efficacious in blocking out any control waves – He also gave me another drug which, if injected into a subject, would enable me to occupy his body for a few hours and only at night 'Don't let the sun come up on you or it's curtains – zero eaten by crab – And now there is the matter of my fee.'

I handed him a brief case of bank notes and he faded into the shadows furtive and seedy as an old junky.

The paper and the embassy had warned me that I would be on my own, a thousand years from any help – I had a vibrating camera gun sewed into my fly, a small tape recorder and a transistor radio concealed in a clay pot – I took a plane to Merida where I set about contacting a 'broker' who could put me in touch with a 'time guide' – Most of these so-called 'brokers' are old drunken frauds and my first contact was no exception – I had been warned to pay nothing until I was satisfied with the arrangements – I found this 'broker' in a filthy hut on the outskirts surrounded by a rubbish heap of scrap iron, old bones, broken pottery and worked flints – I produced a bottle of aguardiente and the broker immediately threw down a plastic cup of the raw spirit and sat there swaying back and forth on a stool while I explained my business – He indicated that what I wanted was extremely difficult – Also dangerous and illegal – He could get into trouble – Beside I might be an informer from the Time Police – He would have to think about it – He drank two more cups of spirit and fell on the floor in a stupor – The following day I called again – He had thought it over and perhaps – In any case he would need a week to prepare his medicines and this he could only do if he were properly supplied with aguardiente – And he poured another glass of spirits slopping full – Extremely dissatisfied with the way things were going I left – As I was walking back towards town a boy fell in beside me.

'Hello, Meester, you look for broker yes? – Muy know good one – Him' he gestured back towards the hut 'No good borracho son bitch bastard – Take mucho dinero – No do nothing – You come with me, Meester.'

Thinking I could not do worse, I accompanied the boy to another hut built on stilts over a pond – A youngish man greeted us and listened silently while I explained what I wanted – The boy squatted on the floor rolling a marijuana cigarette – He passed it around and we all smoked – The broker said yes he could make the arrangements and named a price considerably lower than what I had been told to expect – How soon? – He looked at a shelf where I could see a number of elaborate hour glasses with sand in different colors: red, green, black, blue and white – The glasses were marked with symbols – He explained to me that the sand represented color time and color words – He pointed to a symbol on the green glass 'Then – One hour' – He took out some dried mushrooms and herbs and began cooking them in a clay pot – As green sand touched the symbol, he filled little clay cups and handed one to me and one to the boy – I drank the bitter medicine and almost immediately the pictures I had seen of Mayan artifacts and codices began moving in my brain like animated cartoons – A spermy, compost heap smell filled the room – The boy began to twitch and mutter and fell to the floor in a fit – I could see that he had an erection under this thin trousers – The broker opened the boy's shirt and pulled off his pants – The penis flipped out spurting in orgasm after orgasm – A green light filled the room and burned through the boy's flesh – Suddenly he sat up talking in Mayan – The words curled out his mouth and hung visible in the air like vine tendrils – I felt a strange vertigo which I recognized as the motion sickness of time travel – The broker smiled and held out a hand – I passed over his fee – The boy was putting on his clothes – He beckoned me to follow and I got up and left the hut – We were walking along a jungle path the boy ahead his whole body alert and twitching like a dog – We walked many hours and it was dawn when we came to a clearing where I could see a number of workers with sharp sticks and gourds of seed planting corn – The boy touched my shoulder and disappeared up the path in jungle dawn mist –

As I stepped forward into the clearing and addressed one of the workers, I felt the crushing weight of evil insect control forcing my thoughts and feelings into prearranged moulds, squeezing my spirit in a soft invisible vice – The worker looked at me with dead eyes empty of curiosity or welcome and silently handed me a planting stick – It was not unusual for strangers to wander in out of the jungle since the whole area was ravaged by soil exhaustion – So my presence occasioned no comment – I worked until sun down – I was assigned to a hut by an overseer who carried a carved stick and wore an elaborate head dress indicating his rank – I lay down in the hammock and immediately felt stabbing probs of telepathic interrogation – I turned on the thoughts of a half-witted young Indian – After some hours the invisible presence withdrew – I had passed the first test –

During the months that followed I worked in the fields – The monotony of this existence made my disguise as a mental defective quite easy – I learned that one could be transferred from field work to rock carving the stellae after a long apprenticeship and only after the priests were satisfied that any thought of resistance was forever extinguished – I decided to retain the anonymous status of a field worker and keep as far as possible out of notice –

A continuous round of festivals occupied our evenings and holidays – On these occasions the priests appeared in elaborate costumes, often disguised as centipedes or lobsters – Sacrifices were rare, but I witnessed one revolting ceremony in which a young captive was tied to a stake and the priests tore his sex off with white hot copper claws – I learned also something of the horrible punishments meted out to any one who dared challenge or even think of challenging the controllers: *Death In The Ovens*; The violator was placed in a construction of interlocking copper grills – The grills were then heated to white heat and slowly closed on his body *Death In Centipede*; The 'criminal' was strapped to a couch and eaten alive by giant centipedes – These executions were carried out secretly in rooms under the temple.

I made recordings of the festivals and the continuous music like a shrill insect frequency that followed the workers all day in the fields – However, I knew that even to play these recordings would invite immediate detection – I needed not only the sound track of control but the image track as well before I could take definitive action – I have explained that the Mayan control system depends on the calendar and the codices which contain symbols representing all states of thought and feeling possible to human animals living under such limited circumstances – These are the instruments with which they rotate and control units of thought – I found out also that the priests themselves do not understand exactly how the system works and that I undoubtedly knew more about it than they did as a result of my intensive training and studies – The technicians who had devised the control system had died out and the present line of priests were in the position of some one who knows what buttons to push in order to set a machine in motion, but would have no idea how to fix that machine if it broke down, or to construct another if the machine were destroyed – If I could gain access to the codices and mix the sound and image track the priests would go on pressing the old buttons with unexpected results – In order to accomplish the purpose I prostituted myself to one of the priests – (Most distasteful thing I ever stood still for) – During the sex act he metamorphosed himself into a green crab from the waist up, retaining human arms and genitals that secreted a caustic erogenous slime, while a horrible stench filled the hut – I was able to endure these horrible encounters by promising myself the pleasure of killing this disgusting monster when the time came – And my reputation as an idiot was by now so well established that I escaped all but the most routine control measures –

The priest had me transferred to janitor work in the temple where I witnessed some executions and saw the prisoners torn body and soul into writhing insect fragments by the ovens, and learned that the giant centipedes were born in the ovens from these mutilated screaming fragments – It was time to act – Using the drug the doctor had given me, I took over the priest's body gained access to the room where the codices were kept, and photographed the books – Equipped now with sound and image track of the control machine I was in position to dismantle it – I had only to mix the order of recordings and the order of images and the changed order would be picked up and fed back into the machine – I had recordings of all agricultural operations, cutting and burning brush etc – I now correlated the recordings of burning brush with the image track of this operation, and shuffled the time

so that the order to burn came late and a year's crop was lost –
Famine weakening control lines, I cut radio static into the control
music and festival recordings together with sound and image track
of rebellion

'Cut word lines – Cut music lines – Smash the control images –
Smash the control machine – Burn the books – Kill the priests –
Kill! Kill! Kill! – '

Inexorably as the machine had controlled thought feeling and
sensory impressions of the workers, the machine now gave the
order to dismantle itself and kill the priests – I had the satisfaction
of seeing the overseer pegged out in the field, his intestines
perforated with hot planting sticks and crammed with corn – I
broke out my camera gun and rushed the temple – This weapon
takes and vibrates image to radio static – You see the priests *were*
nothing but word and image, an old film rolling on and on with
dead actors – Priests and temple guards went up in silver smoke as
I blasted my way into the control room and burned the codices –
Earthquake tremors under my feet I got out of there fast, blocks of
limestone raining all around me – A great weight fell from the sky,
winds of the earth whipping palm trees to the ground – Tidal
waves rolled over the Mayan control calendar.

8

I SEKUIN

The Mayan Caper – The Centipede Switch – The Heavy Metal Gimmick

I Sekuin, Perfected These Arts Along The Streets Of Minraud.
Under Sign Of The Centipede. A Captive Head. In Minraud
Time. In The Tattoo Booths. The Flesh Graft Parlors. Living
Wax Work Of Minraud. Saw Thee Dummies Made to Impression.
While You Wait. From Short-Time. In The Terminals Of Min-
raud. Saw The White Bug Juice Spurt From Ruptured Spines. In
The Sex Rooms of Minraud. While You Wait. In Minraud Time.
The Sex Devices Of Flesh. The Centipede Penis. Insect Hairs
Thru Grey-Purple Flesh. Of The Scorpion People. The Severed
Heads. In Tanks Of Sewage. Eating Green Shit. In The Aquari-
ums Of Minraud. The Booths Of Minraud. Under Sign Of The
Centipede. The Sex Rooms And Flesh Films Of Minraud. I
Sekuin A Captive Head. Learned The Drugs of Minraud. In Flak
Braille. Rot Brain And Spine. Leave A Crab Body Broken On
The Brass And Copper Street. I Sekuin Captive Head. Carried
Thru The Booths of Minraud. By Arms. Legs.

Extensions. From The Flesh Works Of Minraud. My Head In
A Crystal Sphere Of Heavy Fluid. Under Sing Sign Of The
Scorpion Goddess. Captive In Minraud. In The Time Booths Of
Minraud. In The Tattoo Parlors Of Minraud. In The Flesh Works
Of Minraud. In The Sex Rooms Of Minraud. In The Flesh Films
Of Minraud. March My Captive Head, Her Captive In Minraud
Time Streets.

On a level plain in the dry sound of insect wings Bradly crash
landed a yellow Cub – area of painted booths and vacant lots – in a
dusty shop window of trusses and plaster feet, a severed head on
sand, red ants crawling through nose and lips – They had this
word dust stirring hot ants all over you.

'You crazy or something walk around alone?'

The guide pointed to the head: 'Guard – You walk through his
eyes and you N.G.' The guide sliced a hand across his genitals
'This bad place, Meester – You ven conmigo – '

He led the way through dusty streets – Metal excrement glowed in corners – Darkness fell in heavy chunks blocking out sections of the city

'Here' said the guide – a restaurant cut from limestone, green light seeping through bottles and tanks where crustaceans moved in slow gyrations – the waiter took their order hissing cold dank breath through a disk mouth

'Good place – cave crabs – Muy bueno for fuck, Johnny – '

The waiter set down a flat limestone shell of squid bodies with crab claws

'Krishnus,' said the guide

Still alive, moving faintly in phosphorescent slime – The guide speared one on a bamboo spike and dipped it into yellow sauce – A sweet metal taste burned through stomach intestines and genitals – Bradly ate the krishnus in ravenous gulps –

The guide raised his arm from the elbow 'Muy bueno, Johnny – You see' The waiter was singing through his disk mouth a bubbling cave song – 'Vamanos, Johnny – I show you good place – We smoke fuck sleep O.K. Muy got good one Johnny – '

Word 'Hotel' exploded in genitals – An old junky took Bradly's money and led them to a blue cubicle – Bradly leaned out a square hole in one wall and saw that the cubicle projected over a void on rusty iron props – The floor moved slightly and creaked under their feet –

'Some time this trap fall – Last fuck for Johnny.'

There was a pallet on the iron floor, a brass tray with hashish pipes, and a stone jar

'Johnny shirt off,' said the guide unbuttoned Bradly's shirt with gentle lush rolling fingers – 'Johnny pants down' – He dipped a green phosphorescent unguent from the jar and smeared it over Bradly's body –

'Smear it on – Smear it in – Johnny me – I Johnny'

He passed the jar to Bradly – 'Now you do say like me.'

'Smear it on – Smear it in – Akid me – I Ahkid – '

A long burn took stomach and intestines – bodies rolled on the pallet leaving trails of flesh – phosphorescent slime sleep –

Woke in stale trade flesh swept out by an old junky coughing and spitting in the sick morning –

This is the way the old hop smoking world I created mutters between years saddest of all movies voices frosted on the glass wind and dust through empty streets and gutted buildings spectral janitors grey autumn chill in the ashes cold dusty halls ... a petition from the old me . . . the narcotics department . . . Colonel Smoky . . . Chinese waiters . . . Pantapon Rose . . . Bill Gains . . . Old Bart . . . Hauser and O'Brien . . . detective junky walk . . . Does he know his old record? (spit blood) 'Bill, it's windy here.' An old junky selling Christmas seals on North Clark St. the 'Priest' they called him.

'Fight tuberculosis folks.'

grey shadow on a distant wall.

9

PRETEND AN INTEREST

Benway 'camped' in the Board of Health. He rushed in anywhere brazenly impounding all junk. He was of course well-known but by adroit face rotation managed to piece out the odds, juggling five or six bureaus in the air thin and tenuous drifting-away cobwebs in a cold Spring wind under dead crab eyes of a doorman in green uniform carrying an ambiguous object composite of club, broom and toilet plunger, trailing a smell of ammonia and scrubwoman flesh. An undersea animal surfaced in his face, round disk mouth of cold grey gristle, purple rasp tongue moving in green saliva: 'Soul Cracker,' Benway decided. species of carnivorous mollusk. exists on Venus. it might not have bones. Time switched the tracks through a field of little white flowers by the ruined signal tower. sat down under a tree worn smooth by others sat there before. We remember the days as long procession of the Secret Police always everywhere in different form. In Guayaquil sat on the river bank and saw a big lizard cross the mud flats dotted with melon rind from passing canoes.

Carl's dugout turned slowly in the brown iridescent lagoon infested with sting-ray, fresh water shark, arequipa, candirus, water boa, crocodile, electric eel, aquatic panther and other noxious creatures dreamed up by the lying explorers who infest bars marginal to the area.

'This inaccessible tribe, you dig, lives on phosphorescent metal paste they mine from the area. Transmute to gold straight away and shit it out in nuggets. It's the great work.'

Liver-sick gold eyes gold maps gold teeth over the Aguardiente cooked on the Primus stove with canella and tea to cut the oil taste leaves silver sores in the mouth and throat.

'That was the year of the Rindpest when all the tourists died even the Scandinavians and we boys reduced to hawk the farter LWR – Local Wage Rate.'

'No calcium in the area you understand. One blighter lost his entire skeleton and we had to carry him about in a canvas bathtub. A jaguar lapped him up in the end, largely for the salt I think.'

Tin boys reduced to hawk the farter the substance and the strata

– You know what that means? – Carried the youth to dead water infested with consent – That was the year of the Clear – local wage rate of Program Empty Body –

'Head Waters of The Baboon-asshole . . . That's Hanging Vine Country – '(The Hanging Vine flicked around the youth's neck moulding to his skull bones in a spiralling tendril motion snapped his neck, he hangs now ejaculating as disk mouths lined with green hairs fasten to his rectum growing tendrils through his body dissolving his bones in liquid gurgles and plops into the green eating jelly.)

'This bad place you write, Meester. You win something like jelly fish.'

They live in translucent jelly and converse in light flashes liquifying bones of the world and eating the jelly – boy chrysalis rotting in the sun – lazy undersea eyes on the nod over the rotting meat vegetable sleep – limestone dope out of shale and water . . .

The youth is hanged fresh and bloody – tall ceremony involves a scorpion head – lethal mating operation from the Purified Ones – no calcium in the area – exists on Venus – it might not have bones – ray moss of orgasm and death – Limestone God a mile away – better than shouts: 'Empty body!' Dead land here you understand waiting for some one marginal to the area.

'Deep in Fucking Drum Country' (The naked initiate is strapped with his back and buttocks fitted to a wooden drum. The drummer beats out orgasm message until the Initiate's flesh lights up with blue flame inside and the drum takes life and fucks the boy ((puffs of smoke across a clear blue sky . . .)) The initiate awoke in other flesh the look-out different . . . And he plopped into squares and patios on 'Write me Meester.')

Puerto Joselito is located at the confluence of two strong brown rivers. The town is built over a vast mud flat criss-crossed by stagnant canals, the buildings on stilts joined by a maze of bridges and cat-walks extend up from the mud flats into higher ground surrounded by tree columns and trailing ianas, the whole area presenting the sordid and dilapidated air of a declining frontier post or an abandoned carnival.

'The town of Puerto Joselito, dreary enough in its physical aspect, exudes a suffocating fog of smoldering rancid evil as if the town and inhabitants were slowly sinking in wastes and garbage. I found these people deep in the vilest superstitions and practices.'

'Various forms of ritual execution are practiced here. These gooks have an aphrodisiac so powerful as to cause death in a total blood spasm leaving the empty body cold and white as marble. This substance is secreted by the species Xiucutl Crustanus, a flying scorpion, during its lethal mating season in the course of which all male Xiucutl die maddened by the substance and will fly on any male creature infecting with its deadly sperm. In one ceremony the condemned are painted as gold, silver, copper and marble statues, then inoculated with Xiucutl sperm their convulsions are channeled by invisible control wires into exquisite ballets and freeze into garden fountains and park pedestals. And this is one of many ceremonies revolving on the Ceremonial Calendar kept by the Purified Ones and the Earth Mother.

'The Purified One selects a youth each month and he is walled into a crystal cubicle moulded on cervical vertebrae. On the walls of the cubicle, sex programs are cut in cuneiforms and the walls revolve on silent hydraulic pressures. At the end of the month the youth is carried through the street on a flower float and ceremonially hanged in the limestone ball court, it being thought that all human dross passes from the Purified One to die in the youth at the moment of orgasm and death. Before the youth is hanged he must give his public consent and if he cannot be brought to consent he hangs the Purified One and takes over his functions. The Purified Ones are officially immortal with monthly injections of youth substance.' Quote Green-Baum Early Explorer.

Carl's outboard vibrated in a haze of rusty oil, bit a jagged piece out of the dugout canoe and sank, in iridescent brown water. somewhere in the distance the muffled jelly sound of underwater dynamite: ('The natives are fishing'). howler monkeys like wind through leaves. A rocket burst over the water and Carl could see people on a board walk flat and stylized as tin targets in a shooting gallery. Metal voices rattled across the water. The dugout twisted slowly and stopped, touching a ruined jetty. Carl got out with his Nordic ruck-sack and walked to the square on high ground. He felt a touch on his shoulder light as wind. A man in mouldy grey police tunic and red flannel underwear one bare foot swollen and fibrous like old wood covered with white fungus, his eyes mahogany color flickered as the watcher moved in and out. He gasped out the word 'Control' and slipped to the ground. A man in grey hospital pyjamas eating handfuls of dirt and trailing green spit crawled over to Carl and pulled at his pants cuff. Another moves forward on brittle legs breaking little puffs of bone meal. His eyes

63

lit up a stern glare went out in smell of burning metal. From all sides they came pawing hissing spitting:

'Papeles!'

'Documentos!'

'Pasaporte!'

'What is all this scandal?' The Commandante in clean khaki was standing on a platform overlooking the square. Above him was an elaborate multi-leveled building of bamboo. His shirt was open on a brown chest smooth as old ivory. A little pistol in red leather cover crawled slowly across his skin leaving an iridescent trail of slime.

'You must forgive my staff if they do not quite measure up to your German ideal of spit and polish . . . backward . . . uninstructed . . . each living all alone and cultivating his little virus patch . . . They have absolutely nothing to do and the solitude . . .' He tapped his forehead. His face melted and changed under the flickering arc lights.

'But there must be thirty of them about,' said Carl.

The Commandante gave him a sharp look. 'They are synchronized of course. They can not see or even infer each other so all think he is only police officer on post. Their lines you sabe never cross and some of them are already . . .'

'And some of them are already dead. This is awkward since they are not legally responsible. We try to bury them on time even if they retain intact protest reflex. Like Gonzalez the Earth Eater. We bury him three times.' The Commandante held up three fingers sprouting long white tendrils. 'Always he eat way out. And now if you will excuse me the soccer scores are coming in from the Capital. One must pretend an interest.'

'318 known dead in Lima soccer riot . . . panic in the stadium . . . 323 dead . . .'

The Commandante had aged from remote crossroads of time crawled into a metal locker and shut the door whimpering with fears, emerged in a mouldy green jock strap his body painted I-Red, U-Green. The assistant flared out of a broom closet high on ammonia with a green goatee and marble face. He removed Carl's clothes in a series of locks and throws. Carl could feel his body move to the muscle orders. The assistant put a pail over his head and screamed away into distant hammers.

The Commandante spread jelly over Carl's naked paralyzed body. The Commandante was moulding a woman. Carl could feel his body draining into the woman mould. His genitals dissolving, tits swelling as the Commandante penetrated applying a few touches to face and hair – (jissom across the mud wall in the dawn sound of barking dogs and running water –) Down there the Commandante going through his incantations around Carl's empty body. The body rose presenting an erection, masturbates in front of the Commandante. Penis flesh spread through his body bursting in orgasm explosions granite cocks ejaculate lava under a black cloud boiling with monster crustaceans. Cold grey undersea eyes and hands touched Carl's body. The Commandante flipped him over with sucker hands and fastened his disk mouth to Carl's asshole. He was lying in a hammock of green hair, penis-flesh hammers bursting his body. Hairs licked his rectum, spiraling tendrils scraping pleasure centers, Carl's body emptied in orgasm after orgasm, bones lit up green through flesh dissolved into the disk mouth with a fluid plop. He quivers red now in boneless spasms, pink waves through his body at touch of the green hairs.

The Commandante stripped Carl's body and smeared on green jelly nipples that pulled the flesh up and in. Carl's genitals wither to dry shit he sweeps clear with a little whisk broom to white flesh and black shiny pubic hairs. The Commandante parts the hairs and makes incision with a little curved knife. Now he is modeling a face from the picture of his novia in the Capital.

'And now, how you say, "the sound effects."' He puts on a record of her voice, Carl's lips follow and the female substance breathed in the words.

'Oh love of my alma! Oh wind of morning!'

'Most distasteful thing I ever stand still for.' Carl made words in the air without a throat, without a tongue. 'I hope there is a Farmacia in the area.'

The Commandante looked at him with annoyance: 'You could wait in the office please.'

He came out putting on his tunic and strapping on a Luger.

'A drug store? Yes I creo ... Across the lagoon ... I will call the guide.'

On a stranded iron boat the guide pointed ...

'There Farmacia Meester.'

A Chinese came out in rusty felt slippers ...

'No glot. Clom Fliday.'

He clanged an iron door and the sign Farmacia fell off the boat and sank in black ooze.

Carl walked through a carnival city along canals where giant pink salamanders and goldfish stirred slowly, penny arcades, tattoo booths, massage parlors, side shows, blue movies, processions, floats, performers, pitchmen to the sky.

Puerto Joselito is located dead water. inactive oil wells and mine shafts, strata of abandoned machinery and gutted boats, garbage of stranded operations and expeditions that died at this point of dead land where sting-rays bask in brown water and crabs walk the mud flats on brittle stilt legs. The town crops up from the mud flats to the silent temple of high jungle streams of clear water cut deep clefts in yellow clay and falling orchids endanger the traveller.

In a green savannah stand two vast penis figures in black stone, legs and arms vestigial, slow blue smoke rings pulsing from the stone head. A limestone road winds through the pillars and into the city. a rack of rusty iron and concrete set in vacant lots and rubble, dotted with chemical gardens. A smell of junky hat and death about the town deadens and weight these sentences with 'disgust you to see it'. Carl walked through footpaths of a vast shanty town. A dry wind blows hot and cold down from Chimborazi a soiled postcard in the prop blue sky. Crab men peer out of abandoned quarries and shag heaps some sort of vestigial eye growing cheek bone and a look about them as if they could take root and grow on anybody. muttering addicts of the orgasm drug, boneless in the sun, gurgling throat gristle, heart pulsing slowly in transparent flesh eaten alive by the crab men.

Carl walked through the penis posts into a town of limestone huts. A ring of priests sat around the posts legs spread, erections pulsing to flicker light from their eyes. As he walked through the electric eyes his lips swelled and his lungs rubbed against the soft inner ribs. He walked over and touched one of the priests and a shock threw him across the road into a sewage ditch. Maize fields surround the town with stone figures of the Young Corn God erect penis spurting maize shoots looks down with young cruelty and innocent lips parted slightly terminal caress in the dropping eyes. The Young Corn God is led out and his robes of corn silk stripped from his body by lobster priests. A vine rope is attached to the stone penis of the Maïs God. The boy's cock rises iridescent in the morning sun and you can see the other room from there by a mirror on the wardrobe . . . Well now, in the city a group of them came to this valley grow corn do a bit of hunting fishing in the river.

Carl walked a long row of living penis urns made from men whose penis has absorbed the body with vestigial arms and legs breathing through purple fungoid gills and dopping a slow metal excrement like melted solder which forms a solid plaque under the urns stand about three feet high on rusty iron shelves wire mesh cubicles joined by cat walks and ladders a vast warehouse of living penis urns slowly transmuting to smooth red terracotta. Others secrete from the head crystal pearls of lubricant that forms a shell of solid crystal over the red penis flesh.

A blast of golden horns: The Druid Priest emerges from the Sacred Grove, rotting bodies hang about him like Spanish moss. His eyes blue and cold as liquid air expand and contract eating light.

The boy sacrifice is chosen by erection acclaim. universal erection feeling for him until all prick point to 'Yes, Boy' feels the 'Yes' run through him and melt his bones to 'Yes' stripped naked in the Sacred Grove shivering and twitching under the Hanging Tree green disk mouths sucking his last bone meal. He goes to the tree naked on flower floats through the obsidian streets red stone buildings and copper pagodas of the fish city stopping in Turkish Baths and sex rooms to make blue movies with youth. The entire city is in heat during this ceremony, faces swollen with tumescent purple penis flesh. Lightning fucks flash on any street corner leave a smell of burning metal blue sparks up and down the spine. a vast bath-town of red clay cubicles green crab boys disk mouth's slow rasping tongue on spine centers twisting in the warm black ooze.

Noteworthy is The Glazing Ceremony when certain of the living urns are covered with terracotta and baked in red brick ovens by the women who pull the soft red meat out with their penis forks and decorate house and garden with the empty urns. The urnings for the Glazing Ceremony are chosen each day by locker number from the public urn and numbers read out over the soft speaker inside the head. helpless urns listening to the number-call charge our soft terror-eating substance, our rich substance.

Now it is possible to beat the number before call by fixing The urn or after call by the retroactive fix which few are competent to practice. There is also a Ceremonial Massage in which the penis flesh is rubbed in orgasm after orgasm until Death in Centipede occurs. Death in Centipede is the severest sentence of the Insect Court and of course all urnings are awaiting sentence for various male crimes. Pués, every year a few experienced urnings beat the house and make Crystal Grade. When the crystal cover reaches a certain thickness the urning is exempt from ceremonial roll call and becomes immortal with nothing to do but slowly accrete a thicker cover in the Crystal Hall of Fame.

Few beat the house. a vast limestone bat. high mountain valley cut off by severest sentence of symbiotic cannibalism. so the game with one another.

'I dunno me. Only work here. Technical Sergeant.'

'Throw it into wind Jack.'

A pimp steps out of him and leans in through the Country Club window. 'Visit the House of David boys and watch the girls eat shit. Makes a man feel good all over. Just tell the madame a personal friend of mine.' He drops a cuneiform cylinder into the boy's hip pocket feeling his ass with lost tongue of the penis urn people in a high mountain valley of symbiotic cannibalism. The natives are blond and blue-eyed sex in occupation. It is unlawful to have orgasm alone and the inhabitants live in a hive of sex-rooms and flickering blue movie cubicles. You can spot one on the cubicle sky line miles away. We all live in the blue image forever. The cubicles fade out in underground steam baths where lurk the Thurlings, malicious boy spirits fugitive from the blue movies who mislead into underground rivers (the traveller is eaten by aquatic centipedes and carnivorous underwater vines).

Orgasm death spurts over the flower floats – Limestone God a mile away – descent into penis flesh cut off by a group of them came to this game under the hanging tree – insect legs under red Arctic night – He wore my clothes and terror –

The boy ejaculates blood over the flower floats. Slow vine rope drops him in a phallic fountain. wire mesh cubicles against the soft inner ribs. vast warehouse of penis and the shock threw him ten feet to smooth dirt and flak. god with erect penis spurting crystal young cruelty and foe solid. dazzling terminal caress in silent corridors of Corn God. erection feeling for descent in the morning sun feels the 'Yes' from there by a mirror on you stripped naked. In the city a group of them came to this last bone meal under the hanging tree.

The priests came through the limestone gates playing green flutes: translucent lobster men with wild blue eyes and shells of flexible copper. A soundless vibration in the spine touched center of erection and the natives moved toward the flute notes on a stiffening blood tube for the Centipede Rites. A stone penis body straddles the opening to the cave room of steam baths and sex cubicles and the green crab boys who go all the way on any line.

From the living god cock flows a stream of lubricant into a limestone trough green with algae. The priests arrange the initiates into long dog-fuck lines moulding them together with green jelly from the lubricant tanks. Now the centipede skin is strapped on each body a segment and the centipede whips and cracks in electric spasms of pleasure throwing off segments kicking spasmodically uncontrolled diarrhoea spurting orgasm after orgasm synchronized with the flicker lights. Carl is taken by the centipede legs and pulled into flesh jelly dissolving bones – Thick black hair sprouts through his tumescent flesh – He falls through a maze of penny arcades and dirty pictures, locker rooms, barracks, and prison flesh empty with the colorless smell of death –

Cold metal excrement on all the walls and benches, silver sky raining the metal word fall out – sex sweat like iron in the mouth. Scores are coming in. Rate shoe. Pretend an interest.

In a puppet booth the manipulator takes pictures of bored insolent catatonics with eight-hour erections reading comics and chewing gum. the impresario is a bony Nordic with green fuzz on his chest and legs. 'I get mine later with the pictures. I can't touch the performers. Wall of glass you know show you something interesting.'

He pulls aside curtain: school-boy room with a banner and pin-ups. on the bed naked boy puppet reading comics and chewing gum with a slight creak. The manipulator applies oil with a hypo.

Ghost your German. Spit penny arcades, tattoo booths, Nordic processions, human performers, trapeze artists. Whores of all sexes importune from scenic railways and ferris wheels where they rent cubicles, push up man-hole covers in a puff of steam, pull at passing pant cuffs, careen out of The Tunnel Of Love waving condoms of jissom. Old blind queens with dirty peep-shows built into their eye-sockets disguise themselves as penny arcades and feel for a young boy's throbbing cock with cold metal hands, sniff pensively at bicycle seats in Afghan Hound drag, Puerto Joselito is located through legs. ghost slime sitting naked on tattoo booths, brown virus flesh of curse. suffocating town, this. ways to bury explorer.

Old junky street-cleaners push little red wagons sweeping up condoms and empty H caps, KY tubes, broken trusses and sex devices, keif garbage and confetti, mouldy jockstraps and bloody

Kotex, shit-stained color comics, dead kitten and afterbirths, jenshe babies of berdache and junkie.

Everywhere the soft insidious voice of the pitchman delayed action language lesson muttering under all your pillows 'Shows all kinds of masturbation and self-abuse. Young boys need it special.' faded sepia genitals in the drawer of a tattoo parlor . . . silver paper in the wind . . . frayed sounds of a distant city.

10

LAST HINTS

Carl descended a spiral iron stairwell into a labyrinth of lockers, tier on tier of wire mesh and steel cubicles joined by catwalks and ladders and moving cable-cars as far as he could see, tiers shifting interpenetrating swinging beams of construction, blue flare of torches on the intent young faces. lockers room smell of mouldy jockstraps, chlorine and burning metal, escalators and moving floors start stop change course, synchronize with balconies and perilous platforms eaten with rust. ferris wheels silently penetrate the structure, roller coasters catapult through to the clear sky – a young workman walks the steel beams with the sun in his hair out of sight in a maze of catwalks and platforms where coffee fires smoke in rusty barrels and the workers blow on their black cotton gloves in the clear cold morning through to the sky beams with sun in his hair the workers blow on their cold morning, dropped down into the clicking turnstiles. buzzers, lights and stuttering torches smell of ozone. breakage is constant. whole tiers shift and crash in a yellow cloud of rust, spill boys masturbating on careening toilets, iron urinals trailing a wake of indecent exposure, old men in rocker chairs screaming anti-fluoride slogans, a southern senator sticks his fat frog face out of the outhouse and brays with inflexible authority: 'and ah advocates the extreme penalty in the worst form there is for anyone convicted of trafficking in, transporting, selling or caught out using the narcotic substance known as nutmeg . . . I wanna say further that Ahm a true friend of the Nigra and understand all his simple wants. Why, I got a good Darkie in here now wiping my ass.'

Wreckage and broken bodies litter the girders, slowly collected by old junkies pushing little red wagons patient and calm with gentle larcenous old woman fingers. Gathering blue torch flares light the calm intent young worker faces.

Carl descended a spiral iron smell of ozone. breakage is of lockers tier on tier of crash in yellow cloud as far as he could see of indecent exposure on toilets. Swinging beams construct the intent young faces.

Locker room toilet on five levels seen from the ferris wheel.

flash of white legs, shiny pubic hairs and lean brown arms, boys masturbating with soap under rusty showers form a serpent line beating on the lockers, vibrates through all the tiers and cubicles unguarded platforms and dead-end ladders dangling in space, workers straddling beams beat out runic tunes with shiny ball-pen hammers. The universe shakes with metallic adolescent lust. The line disappears through a green door slide down to the subterranean baths twisting through torch flares the melodious boy-cries drift out of ventilators in all the locker rooms, barracks, schools and prisons of the world.

'Paco!'

'Joselito!'

'Henrique!'

Carl passed through a barrier of white fog eggs puffs of dust in a grey room filled with funeral urns the recorder twisting a slow tape crumbling to metal word dust fallout on the terminal cities. Word dust dirties his body falling through the space between worlds.

Jacking off he is whiff stateroom that is always kept locked – ('The Van Allen Belt' . . . barely audible click) And word dust dirtied his body falling through the space between worlds –

The third keif pipe he went through the urinal sick and dizzy. He just down from the country. He just down from the green place by the dog's mirror. Sometimes came to a place by the dogs . . . jungle sounds and smells drift from his coat lapels. a lovely Sub that boy.

Ghosts of Panama clung to our bodies – 'You come with me, Meester?' – on the boy's breath a flesh – His body slid from my hands in soap bubbles – We twisted slowly to the yellow sands, traced fossils of orgasm –

'You win something like jelly fish, Meester.'

under a ceiling fan, naked and sullen, stranger color through his eyes the look out different – fading Panama photos swept out by an old junky coughing spitting in the sick dawn –

(phosphorescent metal excrement of the city – brain eating birds patrol the iron streets.)

hospital smell of dawn powder – dead rainbow post cards swept out by an old junky in backward countries.

'I don't know if you got my last hints as we shifted commissions, passing where the awning flaps from the Cafe de France – Hurry up – Perhaps Carl still has his magic lantern – Dark overtakes someone walking – I don't know exactly where you made this dream – Sending letter to a coffin is like posting it in last terrace of the garden – I would never have believed realms and frontiers of light exist – I'm so badly informed and totally green troops – B.B., hurry up please – blackout falling.'

(Stopped suddenly to show me a hideous leather body) – 'I'm almost without medicine.'

It was still goodbye then against the window outside 1920s movie, flesh tracks broken – Sitting at a long table where the doctor couldn't reach and I said: 'He has your voice and end of the line – Fading breath on bed showing symptoms of suffocation – I have tuned them out – How many plots have been forestalled before they could take shape in boy haunted by the iron claws? – Meanwhile a tape recorder cuts old newspapers'. excrement at the far end of forgotten streets – hospital smell on the dawn wind –

(Peeled his phosphorescent metal knees, brain broiled in carrion hunger.)

On the sea wall under fading Panama photo casual ghost of adolescent T-shirt traced fossil-like jelly fish –

'On the sea wall if you got my last hints over the tide flats – I don't know exactly where – woke up in other flesh – shirt with Chinese characters – breeze from the Cafe de France – lantern burning insect wings – I'm almost without medicine – far away – storms – crackling sounds – nothing here now but the circling albatross – dead postcard waiting a place forgotten – '

On the sea wall met a boy under the circling albatross – Peeled his red and white T-shirt to brown flesh and grey under like ash and passed a joint back and forth as we dropped each other's pants and he looked down face like Mayan limestone in the kerosene lamp sputter of burning insect wings 'I screw Johnny up ass.' He jumped with his knees on the bed and slapped his thighs 'asi como perros.' ass hairs spread over the tide flats woke up in other flesh the look out different one boy naked in Panama dawn wind.

11

WHERE THE AWNING FLAPS

'So we got our rocks off permutating through each other's facilities on the blue route and after a little practice we could do it without the projector and perform any kinda awful sex act on any street corner behind the blue glass stirring the passing rectums and pubic hairs like dry leaves falling in the pissoir "J'aime ces types vicieux qu'ici montrent la bite – "'

Drinking from his eyes the idiot green boys plaintive as wind through leaves erect wooden phallus on the graves of dying Lemur Peoples.

'Fluck flick take any place. Johnny you-me-neon-asshole-amigos-now.'

'You only get a hard-on with my permission.'

'Who you now Meester? Flick fluck take Johnny over. Me screw Johnny up same asshole? You me make flick-fluck-one-piece?'

Just hula hoop through each other to idiot Mambo. Every citizen of the area has a blue-print like some are electricals and some are vegetable walking carbonics and so on, it's very technical. boy jissom tracks through rectal mucous and Johnny.

'One track out so: panels of shadow.'

'Me finish Johnny night.'

So we get our rectums in transparent facilities blue route process together. slow night to examine me. both awful sex act on every dawn smell fingers the passing rectum. finger on all cocks: 'I-you-me in the pissoir of present time.' 'Idiot fuck you-me-Johnny. Take.' Leaves erect wood phallus on the me and so on out into a Lemur people 'Flick Fluck idiot asshole buddies like a tree frog clinging in permission. Who are you green hands? fungoid purple?'

'Johnny over. Me screw. Flick fluck one piece.'

Warm spermy smell to idiot Mambo. silence belches smell of ozone and rectal flight: 'Here goes examiner other rectums naked in Panama.'

'Asi' Ass hairs spread over the tide flats. woke up in other flesh, the look out different, one boy naked in Panama dawn wind.

Casual adolescent of urinals and evening flesh gone when I woke up – Age flakes fall through the pissoir – Ran into my old friend Jones – so badly off – forgotten coughing in 1920 movie – Vaudeville voices hustle on bed service – I nearly suffocated trying on the boy's breath – That's Panama – Brain-eating birds patrol the low frequency brain waves – nitrous flesh swept out by your voice and end of receiving set – Sad hand tuned out the stale urine of Panama.

'I am dying, Meester? – forgotten coughing in 1920 street?'

Genital pawn ticket peeled his stale underwear, shirt flapping whiffs of young hard-on – brief boy on screen laughing my skivies all the way down – whispers of dark street in Puerto Assis – Meester smiles through the village wastrel – Orgasm siphoned back telegram: 'Johnny pants down.' (that stale summer dawn smell in the garage – vines twisting through steel – bare feet in dog's excrement –)

Panama clung to our bodies from Las Palmas to David on camphor sweet smell of cooking paregoric – Burned down the republic – The druggist no glot clom Fliday – Panama mirrors of 1910 under seal in any drugstore – He threw in the towel morning light on cold coffee stale breakfast table – little cat smile – pain and death smell of his sickness in the room with me – three souvenir shots of Panama City – Old friend came and stayed all day

'You come with me, Meester?'

And Joselito moved in at Las Playas during the essentials – Stuck in this place – iridescent lagoons, swamp delta, bubbles of coal gas still be saying 'A ver, Luckees' a hundred years from now – a rotting teak wood balcony propped up Ecuador.

'Die Flowers and Jungle bouncing they can't city?'

On the sea wall two of them stood together waving – Age flakes coming down hard here – Hurry up – another hollow ticket – Don't know if you got my last hints trying to break out of this numb dizziness with Chinese characters – I was saying over and over shifted commissions where the awning flaps in your voice – end of the line – silence out there beyond the gate – casual adolescent shirt flapping in the evening wind –

'Old photographer trick wait for Johnny – Here goes Mexican cemetery.'

On the sea wall met a boy with red and white striped T-shirt – (P.G. town in the purple twilight) – The boy peeled off his stale underwear scraping erection – warm rain on the iron roof – under the ceiling fan stood naked on bed service – bodies touched electric – contact sparks tingled – fan whiffs of young hard-on washing adolescent T-shirt – The blood smells drowned voices and end of the line – That's Panama – sad movie drifting in islands of rubbish, black lagoons and fish people waiting a place forgotten – fossil honky tonk swept out by a ceiling fan – Old photographer trick tuned them out

'I am dying, Meester?'

Flashes in front of my eyes naked and sullen – rotten dawn wind in sleep death rot on Panama photo where the awning flaps.

I had as usual been railroaded into the most expensive hotel 3 p.m. eating lunch in the ornate gloomy dining room a bad lunch of many courses the room almost empty . . . a rich family sitting by the window bottles of medicine on the table a commercial traveller in one corner reading the soccer scores.

Then a young man came in and without waiting to be directed by the head waiter sat down at the next table right opposite me you understand in this type dining room the guests are normally spaced out as far as possible an average distance of 23 feet. He was poorly dressed his white shirt very dirty his tie open. Two waiters converged on his table. They did not as I had expected ask him to leave. They took his order with respect and the smiling affection reserved for special clients. I had finished lunch and was smoking a cigarette when he walked over to my table.

'I am Henrique de Santiago. May I join you for coffee?'

Without waiting for my answer he sat down not in a rude or objectionable manner but as if he belonged there looking at me with a familiar smile. He was in his middle twenties very muscular the cheap black suit tight over his biceps. He told me at once in French that he was of the milieu the underworld but son of a well known family in Santiago one hour – he held up a dirty forefinger from the capital. That would explain the waiter's respect. Rich people may dress as they like and if it pleases them to play at being gangsters there is room for that as well. 'I am also a Negro' he added in English 'a smoke.'

I shrugged. Mixed blood is very common in Latin America. The waiter brought coffee and I noticed that he looked like Henrique de Santiago. Come to think of it the entire staff of the hotel looked like Henrique de Santiago.

'You must visit my mother in Santiago and see the coffee plantations.' He wrote something on a slip of paper and handed it to me across the table. He had written on a sheet of yellow note paper 'Monica Cocuera de Santiago Los Fuentes'

'She is known as the "Black Mamba". You will find each other interesting. I myself cannot leave the capital during the season. Besides I am complicated in a matter of stupifying drugs very big you understand.' 'unfortunately' died unuttered as if some one had placed a slow cool finger over my lips. I sat there dreamy and absent looking out of the window across a square empty in the afternoon sun a dog sniffing on the quai seeing all this sharp and clear as if through a telescope warehouses customs sheds and piers of the port the sea ahead. A crescent of land encircled the harbor. I could see a road there and a truck that seemed to be moving very slowly my eyes following the truck. In another few seconds the truck would reach the point. There was a building on the point I could trace its shadowy outlines at the edge of my vision. I turned my head slightly to the left and looked at where the building had been a sheet of silver flame. I threw myself sideways out of the chair floating down very slowly it seemed I saw the dog dragging its hindquarters . . . dust and smoke swept across the square and I hit the floor in a shower of broken glass.

The building I never quite saw was the armory . . . 223 dead . . . thousands injured . . . whole water front quarter of the town destroyed by the explosion. I do not know what happened to Henrique de Santiago. There were many Henriques and many Santiagos in the list of dead. My own injuries were slight as usual and I was discharged from the hospital two days later. I had lost my luggage but I was traveling light an overnight bag a few purchases might as well have a look at Santiago. I hired a cab and asked the driver if he knew Los Fuentes de Santiago. The driver shrugged.

'There is a fountain si in the Plaza but it is dry at this season.' The town was inland from the capital in the foothills white road dusty trees. I told the driver to take me to a hotel of the medium class decent inexpensive large room with a balcony opening onto the Plaza red tile floors brass bed. I went out and walked around the Plaza dusty youths the dry fountain long empty noon awning flaps there in the wind; Cafe de los Fuentes. While I was drinking my coffee a grey anonymous man put a slip of paper on the table. I glanced down . . . yellow circular: Hoy Estreno al Cine Espana . . . La Mamba Negra con Paco, Joselito, Henrique . . . huge black snake reared to strike man in shorts reaching for his pistol . . . at 7 and 10 ... (This circular should appear on the page). I put the circular in my breast pocket intending to catch the 7 o'clock performance. After lunch at the hotel I retired to my room closed the shutters and lay down to sleep. I was awakened by three loud knocks at the door

'Quien es?' I called my voice muffled and distorted. The room was dark. I got out of bed and crossed the room my feet like blocks of wood. I opened the door. A thin figure fully eight feet tall stood there in a long black overcoat. I looked up high cheek bones a face as black as the coat. I could not be sure whether it was a man or a woman.

'I don't know you.' I said in the same muffled voice.

The figure did not speak aloud but the words were there between us 'I know you. See you Sunday.'

The figure disappeared down the stairwell which was round and twisted around the elevator shaft. I closed the door. The catch was broken so I locked the door from the inside with a key I found in a pyjama pocket. I had gone to sleep in underwear shorts. Even in the dim light I could see this was not the hotel room in Santiago. And this was not my old body. Well that would explain the wooden feeling and the distorted voice. I had attempted to force my reactive patterns on another body. I had been too forward. Perceiving my error I moved back. The body regained ease and grace of movement but his heart was pounding. He switched on the light.

I spoke distinctly spelling out the words in English.

'Who was that at the door?'

'There was no one at the door. I had a dream.'

He was not surprised to find someone there in his body. Obviously he had experienced such visits before. I surmised the figure at the door had visited him once and that visit had frightened him so he could not remember. No use to press the matter at this point. I looked around. It was a typical garconniere a compact kitchen at one end of the room a double bed sofa and chairs in cheap imitation of Swedish modern, a door which I surmised led to the bathroom. My host was a young man about 20. He was still upset by his 'dream' so he made a cup of Nescafe and sat down on the sofa smoking a cigarette. I sat there in him and listened. Yes this body had received a lot of visitors ... pieces of finance on the afternoon wind ... tin shares in Buenos Aires ... deals across the table in Lip's ... playboys pretending to be drunker than they were hard alert eyes ... Rome ... Hollywood ... all from the haute monde or marginal to it so far as I could see or hear which is pretty far I am an old visitor from back but this was not in my area at all reason for being here shirt open on the golf course. Quite by chance the same stranger here? hummmrich and powerful visitors but the young man was not rich money is something you can feel as soon as you settle in the spine you can feel it like age or youth junk or sickness a cold grey glaze over everything that's big money and it wasn't here. He was not poor either and the thought of selling himself for money would have outraged him.

'I know nothing whatever about *prostitution*!' these words from a young man I visited long ago he hadn't changed much you don't unless you have to so not rich and not poor yet here he is a walking hotel of wealth and influence adds up his folks run a fancy hotel.

At this point my host spoke in the supercilious tones I was to hear often enough in the days that followed. 'Allow me to introduce your new self. I am Jean Emile Leblanc. My mother is Swedish and my father French. We run a Swedish restaurant in Paris and during the season a resort hotel in Corsica very exclusive. I doubt if they would let you in' trying to needle me is he? I said nothing. 'Who are you?' I said nothing. I am an unobtrusive visitor until I come to the point of my visit you would hardly know I am there.

'Don't talk until you survey the area and figure the action.' The District Supervisor told me there in a shabby office years of grey pain in his eyes long long time you could tell by the shoulders 'What are you some CIA slob? How *they* like to talk chewing it around like a cow with the aftosa and about as dangerous to other human cattle must protect the natives that's what we are here for and small thanks we get for it as you well know.'

'Charming Arab house in the suburbs magic street leaf shadows on the wall the old porter from Arabian Nights friendly nabors invite us in for chicken cous cous and other Moroccan delicacies' cold stale room smell of kerosene heaters that sputter and smoke hostile locals stoning the house screaming Moroccan pleasantries at the door rain outside the roof leaks whiffs of the clogged toilet green mold on my shoes yes I well knew the thanks we get. 'In the immortal words of Dutch Schultz D.S. of the New York area and that's a pretty important job Demolition 23 "Shut up you gotta big mouth!" Bradly and that's for keeping it shut' So he shoves five clams of Havana into my bim and goes into his Luce act. He makes these jokes to ease the pain I guess but it's pretty boring for the kids in the office the 'Chemical Corn Bank' we call him one time he calls me in and there he is writing in long hand dressing gown floppy black slippers a *beret* yet marmite simmering beside him which he is tasting every now and then between sentences with a long wooden spoon. So he bows over the spoon and says

'I am Anatole France le vieux cadavre de France. Your assignment *resuscitate me*!'

and he does a prat fall I have to give him the kiss of life most distasteful thing I ever bent down for and he's got a bank full of this corn and I wanta tell you Bradly from all the kids in office you radioactive old bore any planet would blow up listening to you. A million years he takes to turn his gags to lead this Uranian shit house. *'Bring on the nova and shut Bradly up for the love of Uranus!'*

However I had already opened my big mouth at the door. 'Ah so you prefer to remain the unknown and probably for good reason. Are you a queer? I hate them.'

He got up stretched and yawned. He frowned and put a hand to his head went into the bathroom and took two Veganine tablets and I saw in the mirror he hadn't changed much subject to headaches morning light in the room someone knocking at the door. He puts on a blue dressing gown and opens the door slim model there long yellow hair photo grey eyes

'Hi Fi!'

'Long John!'

(The D.S. retched into his handkerchief.)

They embrace this 'Hi Fi' and 'Long John' yet and the shallow water came in with the tide and the Swedish river of Gothenberg that compost heap smell of sex changing Swedes. She makes coffee chattering away like a bird vibrating every throat for miles around she is a real throat walker that chick a little salute when she stands there bare assed and leans a pert little kiss they do it on all fours dog fashion in the climax throw back their heads and howl 'Is it going to be published in Vogue?' They dress and dance a few records 'High Fi' making the selections with shrill cries shake the fillings out of your teeth so off to the beach in his Folkswagon where I meet Mitzi and Bernard.

Now you would think I found all this boring? Not at all. A visitor is never bored. You see what is boring is getting from here to there custom stops the laundry the post office shaving washing dressing packing looking for a hotel. I didn't have to do any of these things. Jean did it all for me. Visiting is so comfortable and habit forming.

Visiting *is* junk and junk is the oldest visitor in the industry I know what it is to kick a host habit yes that's me there dim flickering on the tele from Spain. They all went away. No good. No bueno. Got time for a coffee kid? I'll tell you a story vacant lot there by the florist shop tin can flash flare a young man waiting cobble stone street smell of ashes he was red haired his face streaked with coal dust.

'Cigarette Mister?'

My contact there sun cold on a thin boy with freckles fading streets a distant sky ... sewage canal smell of coal gas black out falling ... its windy here sweating fear like a vice ... distant blurred 1920 street. 'Here comes the old pencil man.'

a creased red face a cheap blue suit 'So remember the shabby quarters.' Outline of his body guard there grey suit brown face pencil gun ready

'Razor blades ... shoe laces ... arm bands ... pencils ... chalk ... sealing wax ...'

'We'll be wanting two pencils' I said there on North Clark St. trying to get at my shoulder holster.

'Two yellow pencils from Pitman's Common Sense Arithmetic never came out at recess time that afternoon I watched the torn sky bend with the wind ... a thin boy with freckles ... You know how to push this pencil, kid?

pencil kid? the "Grey Pencil" here trained with Ma Currie in the little blue school house we called her "Mother" wouldn't you taught me everything I am.' years of grey pain long long time you could tell by the shoulders. 'I'll say it country simple from Pitman's Common Sense Arithmetic the lead in this pencil used to be radium a million radio active years here in this pencil draw it all the way back now push the pencil ... *nobody there* distant 1920 wind and dust ... Mrs. Murphy's rooming house remember it was a long time ago but not too far to walk there it is just ahead red brick building on a corner of the alley from the attic room you look across the playground of the orphanage with a telescope you can watch the boys at tall black windows of the dormitory a shock to see the boys I was diseased there now pieces of mutilated self blurred yellow ribs torn across the playground with a telescope "Windy 18" there by the "Cement Mixer" "Dusty Freckles" hugging his knees naked on the shower floor.'

'Shove his legs apart boys!' screamed the Director.

'blurred yellow recess time 1920s sing you a scene between us where time had never written a thin boy looked like me in prep school clothes train whistles to a distant closing dormitory sad old human papers I carry diseased voice so painful telling you "Sparks" is over New York. Have I done the job here? Will he hear it?'

dim jerky far away some one had shut a bureau drawer in the dim attic

'You only use a pencil gun once kid . . . phosphorescent stump of an arm and that was all I had to see him by last light left on a dying star . . . an old junky dunking pound cake in the grey cafeteria a napkin under his coffee the "Priest" they called him sold a special crucifix that glowed in the dark until he glowed in the dark himself cold coffee sitting right where you are sitting now you see son when you get a host habit you forget about other folks . . . the boy waiting there . . . Mrs. Murphy's rooming house . . . all the sad old showmen . . . remember her queer son in the kitchen shaving his chest hairs blowing into the soup and singing away like a bird a musical family remember ah here we are *Rooms To Let* curtains grey as orphanage sugar a grey shadow always peeking out

'Will you be settling your account today Mr. Jones?'

'Yes Mrs. Murphy I'll be settling my account these stairs they'll be the death of me/cough/you only use a pencil gun once remember I am the director of no repeat performance showed you the papers clear as "Annie Laurie" in 1920 movie from a dying star . . . sad young image dripping stagnant flower smell of sickness to a distant window . . . I'll tell you story called the Street of Chance . . . Arab house in the suburbs cold coffee sitting right where you are sitting now it's raining the roof leaks I am moving the sofa to a dry spot heavy Spanish thing when I saw a little dry niche behind the sofa I had not noticed before. In the niche is a book glazed grey cover written in letters of gold long hand "The Street of Chance" I opened the cover'

'Being the story of a 14 year old boy who died during the invasion.'

picture of the boy there faded sepia at the attic window waving to a distant train.

12

THE STREETS OF CHANCE

cool remote cobble stone street fresh southerly winds a long time ago boy there by the stream bare feet twisted on a fence followed a flight of wild geese across a violet evening sky then he was above the stream above the street and the houses looking down on the train tracks with no fear of falling. When he got back to the house he told his father about it in the attic room his father used as a studio.

'I can fly father.'

'We have no such powers my son.'

sad train whistles cross a distant sky blue magic of all movies in remembered kid standing there face luminous at the attic window waving to the train dust on the window a sighing sound back the empty room held a little boy photo in his withered hand cross a distant sky the boy's voice

'long long expected call from you.'

'I wrote son.'

agony to breathe this message agony to remember the words used to be the man you were looking for used to be the man click click click of distant heels back down a shabby street dim grey stairs smell of old pain long long you could tell by his shoulders

'Used to be me Mister. Mrs. Murphy's Rooming House remember'

'Will you be settling your account today?'

silver morning shadows on a distant wall jerky bureau drawer dawn in his eyes on the bed naked there shirt in one hand smell of young nights light years wash over his face sad middle aged smile

'I was waiting there.'

blue magic of all movies in remembered kid standing there fading streets a distant sky. He waves sadly from the Street of Chance. see the vacant film his face.

'Quiet now I go.'

sad middle aged face dim jerky faraway smile.

'I was waiting there'

boy standing by the empty bargain. He waves sadly from the Street of Chance.

Film union sub spirit couldn't find the cobbled road content with an occasional Mexican in the afternoon a body sadness to say goodbye infer his absence as wind and dust in empty streets of Mexico

Iron cell wall paint flaking rust – grifa smoke through the high grate window of blue night

'Two prisoners sit on lower iron shelf bunk smoking. One is American the other Mexican – The cell vibrates with silent blue motion of prison and all detention in time.

'Bueno Johnny?' His fingers flicked Johnny's shirt. They stood up. José hung his shirt on a nail, Johnny passed shirt and José hung one shirt over the other. 'Ven aca.' He caught Johnny's belt-end with one hand and flipped the belt-tongue out and opened fly buttons with pick-pocket fingers.

'Ya duro, Johnny hard.'

'Claro.'

José moved into the bunk on knees: 'Like this Johnny,' he slapped his thighs. 'Come perros.'

the other moved into place

'Johnny like?'

'Mucho.'

'Breathe in deep Johnny.'

They froze there breathing: 'Bueno Johnny?'

'Bueno.'

'Vamanos.' Shadow bodies twisted on the blue wall. 'Johnny sure start now.'

'You is coming Johnny?'

'Siiiiiii.'

'Here goes Johnny.' Spurts cross the surplus blanket smell of iron prison flesh and clogged toilets. squeezing through a maze of penny arcades dirty pictures in the blue Mexican night. The two bodies fell languidly apart bare feet on the army blanket. Grifa smoke blown down over black shiny pubic hairs copper and freckle flesh. Paco's cock came up in smoke.

'Otra vez Johnny?' He put his hands behind Johnny's knees.

'Johnny hear knees now.'

Mexico thighs: 'Como perros I fuck you.'

Walls painted blue smoke through the grate. Finger up Johnny's ass moved two prisoners. He held Johnny's thighs and vibrated silent deep Johnny. His cock slid: 'Johnny, I in.'

'Let's go,' twisted the iron frame. 'Porqué no?'

'Bueno Johnny.' Candle shadow bodies. 'Johnny sure desnudate por completo . . . Johnny?'

'Siiii?'

'Here goes completo.' plus blankets smell of iron and shirt on nail. Mexican pick-pocket one shirt over the other. Spurts maze of dirty pictures. Mexican pants down.

part bare feet on the blanket. black shiny pubic hairs.

'I think like mucho be José – Paco – Henrique.'

'Como perros Johnny like? Breathe José in there deep Johnny.'

His cock iron frame for what not breathing: 'Let's go bunk.'

'You is coming plus Paco.' Cross blanket smell of Johnny flicked one shirt. Go completo plus Kiki. 'You is coming for Johnny.'

One shirt spilling head. The bodies feel cock flip out and up.

'Como eso I fuck you.' One shirt spilling Johnny.

'Fuck on knees. Lie down blanket. Como eso through the iron.' He feel tongue on knees. Smoke fuck on knees.

'Mucho be Angelo como eso.'

'Deep Johnny.'

Shoved white knees. vibrate thighs. 'Flip now.'

'Paco? slow.'

'Si the ass Johnny? I screw Johnny up ass?'

Spurts prison flesh to Mexican night: 'Vibrate, Johnny.'

'Let's go.'

'Johnny knees down. Boca abajo. You is coming como eso?'

'Hard bunk Johnny. Me up in Freckles. Como perros like on knees.'

'I screw Johnny Mexican. Smoke fuck Johnny. Como eso Johnny fuck on knees.'

He feel flipped the knees. 'You is coming otra vez Johnny?' He flipped Johnny. Vaseline the ass. One shirt spilling Johnny flicked out and up.

'One mucho Johnny flip now.'

'Breathe José into hilt ass Johnny.'

'Start now.'

'You is coming?'

Spurts cross calconcillos todo. José hung his prison flesh. feel 'come here.' He caught Johnny belt spine. He feel flipped the belt-tongue cross pick-pocket fingers. The bodies fell languidly. Grifa smoke blown down line. 'A ver like this.' He clipped into the bunk on knees like:

José knees. twisting Johnny's thighs.

'Flip now. José slow deep Johnny.' His cock slid ass Johnny.

'Bueno Johnny?'

Breathing. 'Let's go bunk. Johnny candle shadow now.'

'You is coming por completo.'

'Siiii,' spurts spilling cross bare feet.

(Moving two prisoners in the blue? Is American bunk?)

'Mucho Johnny vibrate blue pressure. Breathe José in there. Si iron frame.'

'Porqué no?'

'Johnny here go completo plus Kiki.' Hung his prison flesh nail.

Johnny spurts cock. pictures.

'Claro you like mucho be Kiki. A ver. Como eso.'

Just hula hoop through each other to idiot Mambo . . . all idiot Mambo spattered to control mechanization

'Salt Chunk Mary' had all the 'nos' and none of them ever meant 'yes'. She named a price heavy and cold as a cop's black jack on a winter night and that was it. She didn't name another. Mary didn't like talk and she didn't like talkers. She received and did business in the kitchen. And she kept it in a sugar bowl. Nobody thought about that. Her cold gray eyes would have seen the thought and maybe something goes wrong on the next lay John Citizen come up with a load of oo buckshot into your soft and tenders or Johnny Law just happens by. She sat there and heard. When you spread the gear out on her kitchen table she already knows where you sloped it. She looks at the gear and a price falls out heavy and cold and her mouth closes and stays shut. If she doesn't want to do business she just wraps the gear up and shoves it back across the table and that is that. Mary keeps a coffee pot and a big iron pot of salt pork and beans always on the wood stove. When you fall in she gets up without a word and puts a mug of coffee and plate of salt chunk in front of you. You eat and then you talk business. Or maybe you take a room for a week to cool off. room 18 on the top floor I was sitting in the top room rose wall paper smoky sun set across the river. I was new in the game and like all young thieves thought I had a licence to steal. It didn't last. Sitting there waiting on the Japanese girl works in the Chink laundry a soft knock and I open the door naked with a hard on it was the top floor all the way up you understand nobody on that landing. 'Ooooh' she says feeling it up to my oysters a drop of lubricant squeezed out and took the smoky sun set on rose wall paper I'd been sitting there naked thinking about what we were going to do in the rocking chair rocks off down the line she could get out of her dry goods faster than a junky can fix when his blood is right so we rocked away into the sun set across the river just before blast off that old knock on the door and I shoot this fear load like I never feel it wind up is her young brother at the door in his cop suit been watching through the key hole and learn about the birds and the bees some bee I was in those days good looking kid had all my teeth and she knew all the sex currents goose for pimple always made her entrance when your nuts are tight and aching a red haired boy smoky rose sun set one bare knee rubbing greasy pink wall paper he was naked with a hard on waiting on the Mexican girl from Marty's a pearl of lubricant squeezed slowly out and glittered on the tip of his cock. There was a soft knock at the door. He got up off the crumpled bed and opened the door. The girl's brother stood there smiling. The red haired boy made a slight choking sound as blood rushed to his face pounded and sang in his ears. The young face there on the landing turned black around the edges. The red haired boy sagged against the door jam. He came to on the bed the Mexican kid standing over him

'All right now? Sis can't come'

The Mexican kid unbuttoned his shirt. He kicked off his sandals dropped his pants and shorts grinning and his cock flipped out half up. The Mexican kid brought his finger up in three jerks and his cock came up with it nuts tight pubic hairs glistening black he sat down on the bed.

'Vaseline?'

The red haired boy pointed to the night table. He was lying on the bed breathing deeply his knees up. The Mexican kid took a jar of vaseline out of a drawer. He kneeled on the bed and put his hands behind the freckled knees and shoved the boy's knees up to his trembling red ears. He rubbed vaseline on the pink rectum with a slow circular pull. The red haired boy gasped and his rectum spread open. The Mexican kid slid his cock in. The two boys locked together breathing in each other's lungs. After the girl left I walk down to Marty's where I meet this Johnson has a disgruntled former chauffeur map indicates where a diamond necklace waits for me wall safe behind the Blue Period. Or maybe you Picasso on Rembrandt and cool off like I was sitting in a

Turner sun set on the Japanese girl doing my simple artisan job hot and heavy. Mary she kept the guide ready her eyes heavy and cold as a cop's come around with the old birds and bees business. Nobody thought about that cold outside agent call. Recall John Citizen came up on her. Johnny Law just happens by magic shop in Westbourne Grove. Smell these conditions of ash? I twig that old knock. Klinker is dead. Blackout fell on these foreign suburbs here

'Be careful of the old man. kinda special deputy carries a gun in the car.'

Music fading in the East St. Louis night broken junk of blue exploded star sad servant of the inland side shirt flapping in a wind across the golf course a black silver sky of broken film precarious streets of yesterday back from shadows the boy solid now I could touch almost you know both of us use the copper lustre basin in the blue attic room now Johnny's back. Who else put a slow cold hand on your shoulder shirt flapping shadows on a wall long ago fading streets a distant sky.

He woke up with the sun in his room Spanish voices from the kitchen stretched arched his body looking down flapping himself he got out of bed naked phallic shadow on a distant wall picked up his red boxer shorts one hand down over his crotch 'Entra!' He stood there looking out the window wash flapping it was Sunday picked up his shirt worn grey flannel pants cracked black shoes boat whistling in the harbor coffee and bread in the kitchen down the stairs past wash on the balconies unlocked his bicycle. Paco was waiting for him sitting on his bicycle by the wire gate of the compound smoking a cigarette

'Que tal, Henrique?'

Kiki accepted a cigarette

'Vamanos para arriba a la punto.'

'Bueno.'

They pedalled out along the sea wall. The road was almost empty a few fishermen. They passed a young man walking red hair un ingles the young man turned and looked as they passed

'Yo pienso que es maricon, Paco. Quieres follarle?'

'Porque no.'

They made a wide U turn and stopped in front of the red haired boy

'Que hora es senor?'

'Son las diez.'

He offered them English cigarettes. The two boys sat there on their bicycles smoking. Paco began to rub his crotch and slowly Kiki did the same. The boy looked from one to other and licked his lips blushing

'Muy caliente, senor ... very hot my friend and I ... We fuck you?'

'Pero donde?'

'Sabemos un lugar. Suba'

He pointed to the handle bar. The boy sat there feeling the cold steel on his buttocks as they pedalled out to the point Kiki squeezed him with his elbows

'Aqui'

They turned off the road locked their bicycles and hid them in some bushes

'Par aqui.'

Up a slope of scrub and limestone was a cave mouth concealed by bushes inside a smell of rusty limestone drawings scratched on the wall.

'Muchos han follado aqui' Paco pointed to the drawings. Kiki took off his shoes he opened his shirt and took off his pants

'Paco vayate a vigilar.'

'Nadie pasa por aqui.'

Paco walked over to the mouth of the cave. He took a cigarette out of his pants pocket and stood there watching the sea. Kiki shoved his shorts down leaning forward. He dropped his shorts on his pants and shirt and stood up. The other boy was naked to his socks. Kiki put his hands on the boy's shoulders.

'Vuelvate' turning him hands on shoulders leaf shadows in the wind over their bodies 'Aganchete'

The boy bent over and put his hands on his knees. There was a red mark on the boy's buttocks from the handle bar. Kiki massaged the mark. Standing with his feet apart Kiki spit in his hand rubbing shoving the boy's cheeks apart hitched his hands around the boy's hips shadows merging twisting on a distant wall two bodies wracked with shuddering gasps. Paco had turned from the mouth of the cave and stood there watching and rubbing his crotch.

'Holé!' he said as the sharp odor of semen spurted from the boy's body. Kiki made a noise like a popping cork and withdrew.

'Hasta aqui, Kiki' Paco pointed with his foot 'Dos metros al menos.' Kiki got a handkerchief out of his pants pocket. He walked over to the mouth of the cave and wiped himself shirt flapping in the wind.

'Yo ahora' said Paco.

The boy leaned against the wall. 'Espera un ratito'

He got the English cigarettes from his shirt pocket Kiki dressed now cigarette smoke drifting out the cave mouth the boy shifted from one foot to the other feeling their eyes on his naked body waiting.

Paco brought his finger up in three jerks. and took off his clothes. He hooked his hands from behind around the boy's shoulders working his body like a pump in the climax Paco held the boy to keep him from falling.

Afterwards he gave them money for a movie and they left him there by his hotel on the sea wall and pedalled away down the slate shore boy voices drifting in the afternoon wind.

'Paco!'

'Joselito!'

'Henrique!'

'La Mamba Negra'

con Paco, Joselito, Henrique

a las 4 de la tarde.

Are you a member of the union? Film Union 4 P.M.? Sunday noon Jean woke up with a migraine head ache. Letting him feel my presence quite clearly I guided him to a Farmacia and put the words in his throat

'Diosan comprimidos'

'Si senor.'

Four codeine tablets with coffee knocked out the head ache. I advised him to stay in his room and see nobody. He was reading an English detective story the Vicar done it if my memory serves big soft unctuous reverend with well manicured hands. 4 P.M. the action starts cold coffee sitting right where you are sitting now tube of codeine tablets unmade bed a glass crusted with tomato juice every object in the room said 'hopeless' so I knew D. (for Dead) White of American Narcotics was there to pay his dues that colorless no-smell of death you can hardly breathe with White in the room dreary as a cigarette butt in cold scrambled eggs on the plate there real as a landlady wanting the rent.

'Will you be settling your account today?'

Yes Mr. White I'll be settling my account today.

'Long John put on the Flying Dutchman and reach me those head phones.'

The music pouring in any second now do or say carefully calculated surface 'Demotition 23 loud and clear

'Wind! Wind! Wind!'

He is taking shape now bald head blue eyes caught in whirlpools of wind his face went black with hate and evil a black shadow fell on the page I stood up and caught the boy to keep him from falling a black shadow there on the wall.

'Moka! Moka! Moka!' the boy screamed

'Stand aside Mr. Lablanc!' I told him.

I was *there* now all the way pencil gun ready the shadow dodged sideways and lashed down. I moved back through a funnel of photo faces grey dawn stairs distant 1920 wind and dust the shadow snapped back to the wall ... *sput! nobody there* just a little hole in the plaster wall white dust drifting afternoon sun do my work and go.

Looks like a door it is the last picture a sea wall getting dark is the boy there? He touched his genitals back along the hand the sea chest click of distant heels back along the slate shore cool Sunday silence last picture boy there on the sea wall he touched his genitals back along the hands there the cold sea chest click distant heels back is the boy there? room far away naked phallic shadow cool Sunday on a distant wall I was blackout hung over cold stale room green mold on my clothes Arab house foreign suburbs here shaving in the kitchen whiffs from the John which is one hole in the floor dirty dishes cigarette butt put out in scrambled eggs

'Who's that at the door? Give him some money. Send him away.'

So up to my work room smell of kerosene gray flaking plaster walls that house *aged* while you wait so I belts down a local drug called Hushuma how can anyone live here without it and called all my sad captains from Ragged Staff Road now standing last review.

'Oh God another beggar at the door.'

'The man is here to read the meter, John, and you know what that means in show biz.'

'So he begins to breathe "heavy duty ... vast army ripped to shreds" It's a cold audience, doc. Summoned we stand.'

'It's a federal summons don't like the suck of this could be interstate commerce our halitosis ads violate the cannons of good taste folk scared to eat from the fear of halitosis banging our

Chloryphie, main line a green thought in a green shade smells like a summer golf course American house rain outside . . . What's wrong with that?'

'It smells to California, doc, 23 Panhandle Door.'

'And God how you stink when you don't get your "Greenies" on time! . . . Ever bang the "White Kid"? pure liquid morality from decent Southern stills, suh, keeps you in the *right* all the time after all those folk in Hiroshima was *wrong* . . . *decent folk* buy *Bradly White* . . . Bradly's broken junk of exploded star . . . It's tough to kick a White, kid killed a heap of folk there crumpled cloth bodies fading streets white out . . .

'Now some like the "Blues" . . . blue mist slate roof thousand dollar bills rustling over the floor . . . Simon aimes tu le bruit des pas sur les feuilles mortes frozen in a blue block of bank notes? Some are Yellow and sit there in the sun like a suave evil Mandarin Cardinal feeds himself on torture films only food of this village an amber staff in his old yellow hands . . .

'Caught the Running Cardinal two flights down. Old Gimp died there in color.'

Some turns purple remember the 'Purple People Eaters' in room 25? Mrs. Murphy's rooming house red brick building on a corner of the alley now reds a nice color strong men cried when we had to suck the lead dog wiping off his face with a red bandana the boy jack off in . . . And Farmer Brown here *doesn't care* if he smells getting his shale and peat bog kicks old experienced outhouse . . .

So choose your color kid. It's all junk. Bradly's broken junk of exploded star. Mrs. Murphy's rooming house remember I was traveling with Pantapon Rose and her was a sporting woman room with rose wall paper her was screaming sexy third day of her kick and Christ she come all out in this purple rash covered with slime and I said 'It looks like a purple people eater with the coke horrors I stabbed her 23 times senores wouldn't you?' just an old showman from Mrs. Murphy's rooming house they called him the 'Old Color Man.' 'Give back the color you stole' didn't leave him much color fading down a funnel of copy faces in the cold spring air a colorless question is the boy there? your little thin boy getting thinner a voice stopped in his mind . . . American house summer golf course waiting for rain

'"Summer Golf Course" waiting for "Rain" . . . Come in please . . .'

'Line went dead end of a subdivision street what a spot to land with a cripple ship train whistle brought crippled boy to a distant window wasn't much I could do there you understand "Sparks" *not there* so remember the shabby quarters Mister ... your old friend room over the florist shop smell of young nights sad old papers I carry remember the "Paper Boy"? sun cold on a thin boy with freckles you have known me for a long time, Mister, leave cigarette money.'

smoke faces.

slow grey film fallout and funeral urns of Hollywood. Never learn? the guide clicked him through a silent turnstile into a cubicle of blue glass and mirrors so that any panel of the room was at alternate intervals synchronized with the client's sex-pulse mirror or wall of glass into the next cell on all sides and the arrangement was an elaborate permutation and very technical ... So Johnny the Guide said: 'The first clause in our blue contract is known as the examination to which both parties must submit ... We call it the probing period, now isn't that cute?'

The guide put on helmet of lens goggles and antennae of orange neon flickering, smelling bat wings: 'Johnny pants down. Johnny cock hard.' He brought his arm up from the elbow swimming in for close-ups of Johnny's erection: take slow and take fast under flickering vowel colors: I Red/U Green/E White/O Blue/A Black/ 'Bend over Johnny.' The examiner floats up from the floor, swims down through heavy water from the ceiling, shoots up from toilet bowl, English baths, underwater takes of genitals and pubic hairs in warm spermy water. The goggles lick over his body phosphorescent moths, through rectal hairs orange haloes flicker around his penis. In his sleep, naked Panama nights, the camera pulsing in blue silence and ozone smells, sometimes the cubicle opens out on all sides into purple space. X-ray photos of viscera and fecal movements, his body a transparent blue fish.

'So that's the examination we call it, sees all your processes. You can't deceive us in any way at all and now you got the right to examine me.'

Lee put on the photo goggles melt in head and saw the guide now blond with brown eyes slender and tilted forward. He moved in for a close-up of the boy's flank and took his shirt off followed the pants down, circled the pubic hair forest in slow autogyros, zeroed in for the first stirrings of tumescence, swooping from the stiffening blood tube to the boy's face, sucking eyes with neon proboscis, licking testicles and rectum. The goggles and antennae fade in smoke and slow street-eyes swim up from grey dust and funeral urns. and in his sleep naked blue movies slow motion. Pulsing blue silence photos genitals and pubic hairs in rectal mucous and carbolic soap. flickering over faded thousand-run faces, hearing, smelling through them like: 'Johnny cock hard.' slow down to statues with catatonic erection slow falling through colors Red Green Black. A hot spread: cheeks close-up. felt over Johnny's body the slow float down from the hot Panama nights, blue cubicle guide had transparent ass. They clicked in through a squat toilet and the bath room with walls of blue glass warm soapy spermy water smell. So felt the boy neon fingers on sex spots breathing through sponge rock penis-flesh and brown intestine jungles lined with flesh-eating vines and frantic parasites of the area . . .

Naked in the Panama night, rectal mucous and carbolic soap. a blue screen guide put on goggles. Pale panels of shadow melted his head on all sides into blue silent wings over the clock of fecal movement smelling through them like transparent.

'A hot spread examination we call it. Johnny's body can't deceive us in any way. Came to the hot Panama nights to examine me.'

Clicked into his head of blue glass. Close-up neon finger over the scar-impressions learning the instrument panels, recording on the transparent flesh of present time. It is happening right now. Slow 1920 finger on the cobra lamps, flickering movie shadows into the blue void. pulling finger rolls a cuneiform cylinder. lens eye drank the boy's jissom in yellow light.

'Now Meester we flick fluck i me you cut.' The two film tracks ran through impression screen. one track flash on other cut out in dark until cut back: 'Me finish Johnny's shit . . . Clom through Johnny . . .' hear rectums merging in flicks and orgasm of mutual processes. and pulsed in and out of each other's body on slow gills of sleep in the naked Panama nights draped over the washstand in East St. Louis junk-sick dawn. smell of carbolic soap and rectal mucous and train whistle wake of blue silence and piss through my cock 'i-you-me-fuck-up-ass-all-same-time-four-eyes.' phantom cleavage crude and rampant. Every Citizen can now grow sex forms in his bidet: in the night of Talara felt his hard-on against my khaki pants as we shifted slots and i browned a strange Danish dog under the nudes of Sweden. warm spermy smell, room of blue glass strung together on light-lines of jissom and shit, shared meals and belches, the shifting of testes and contractions of rectum, flick-fluck back and forth.

'Here goes Johnny. We fluck now first run': in blue silence saw the two one track out: Blue. Each meet image coming round the other erection-fucked-self and came other shit both.

'We flick fluck i-you-film-tracks through rectal mucous and carbolic soap. Cut out pale panels of shadow.' Blue silent bat wings over rectums blending in transparent erection. a hot shit and all process together.

'Johnny's body can't deceive us in other body. Slow night to examine me.' sick dawn smell of carbolic finger. close up finger on all cocks.

'I you-me fuck up neon blind fingers phantom cleavage of boy impressions witch board of present time.'

The idiot green boys leaped on Johnny like tree frogs clinging to his chest with sucker paws fungoid gills and red mushroom penis pulsing to the sex waves from Johnny eyes. warm spermy smell, lamps and flicker movies strung together on a million fingers shared meals and belches and lens-eye drank jissom. contract of rectum flight: 'Here goes Johnny. One flight out.' Screen other rectum naked in Panama night.

Ghost of Panama clung to our throats, coughing and spitting on separate spasms, phosphorescent breath fades in fractured air – sick flesh strung together on a million fingers shared meals and belches – nothing here now but circling word dust – dead postcard falling through space between worlds – this road in this sharp smell of carrion –

· We twisted slowly to black lagoons, flower floats and gondolas – tentative crystal city iridescent in the dawn wind – (Adolescents ejaculate over the tide flats)

In the blue windy morning masturbating a soiled idiot body of cold scar tissue – catatonic limestone hands folded over his yen – a friend of any boy structure cut by a species of mollusk – street boys of the green gathered – slow bronze smiles from a land of grass without memory – cool casual little ghosts of adolescent spasm – metal excrement and crystal glooms of the fish city – under a purple twilight our clothes shredded mummy linen on obsidian floors – Panama clung to our bodies

'You come with me, Meester?'

The green cab boys go all the way on any line

Green boys – idiot irresponsibles – rolling in warm delta ooze fuck in color flashes through green jelly flesh that quivers together merging and drawing back in a temple dance of colors. 'Hot licks us all the way we are all one clear green substance like flexible amber changing color and consistency to accommodate any occasion.'

'This bad place Meester. You crazy or something walk around alone. Where you go?' The guide: impersonal screen swept by color winds light up green red white blue. antennae ears of flexible metal cartilage crackle blue spark messages leaving smell of ozone in the shiny black pubic hairs that grow on the guide's pink skull. blood and nerves hard meat cleaver his whole body would scorn to carry a weapon. and being inside was him and more. face cut by image-flak impersonal young pilot eyes riding light rays pulsing through his head.

'Fluck Johnny? Up ass?' He guided Carl with electric tingles in spine and sex hairs through clicking gates and turnstiles, escalators and cable cars in synchronized motion. impersonal young pilot eyes riding. the blue silence permutated Carl into an iron cubicle with painted blue walls pallet on the floor brass tea-tray keif pipes and jars of phosphorescent green sex paste. wall over the pallet two-way mirrors opposite wall of glass opening on the next cubicle and so on, sex acts into the blue distance. The Guide pointed to the mirror: 'We fuck good Johnny. On air now.'

'Johnny pants down' – he was smearing the sex paste on Johnny's ass hot licking the white nerves and pearly genitals – Carl's lips and tongue swelled with blood and his face went phosphorescent penis purple – slow penetrating incandescent flesh tubes siphoned his body into a pulsing sphere of blue jelly floated over skeletons locked in limestone – The cubicles shifted – Carl was siphoned back through the guide and landed with a fluid plop as the cubicles permutated fucking shadows through ceilings of legs and sex hairs, black spirals of phantom assholes twisting like a Kansas cyclone.

'You come with me Meester?'

Green lizard boy with slow idiot smile poses on the bank of a stagnant stream under a railroad bridge. A sleeping carrion hunger flickers in his eyes one hand rests lightly on his worn leather jock strap. Little naked black boy passes around a greasy skull cap with obscene mocking gestures.

The American tourists shift uneasily from one foot to the other. They are eager to understand native customs but this does seem a bit much. A pink faced man coughs and looks hastily away as the lizard boy rubs his jock strap with one slow finger

'How much should we give?'

'Yes that's enough.'

'I wish we could find some sort of town . . . a decent hotel . . . Mother isn't well.'

The tourists drift vaguely away muttering 'I can't understand why the man from American Express wasn't at the airport to meet us.'

An American boy with red hair named Jerry detached himself from the tourists walked over to the green boy and said 'Var silvin wend?'

The green boy smiled and stroked his bulging jock strap

'What you want Johnny?' said the little black boy 'Me speak good English work American base know Meesters.' He ran his hand down over his crotch and flipped out an erection 'Meester Melican cocksuckers . . . What you want Johnny? Black fruit?'

Jerry blushed and nodded. The black boy turned and said something to the green boy. The green boy stood there smiling and silent 'He think plenty slow . . . no need think much . . . tourist pay plenty justa looka him . . . You got money Johnny? ten dollar American him take off leather.'

Jerry took ten dollars out of his wallet and handed it to the black boy. The black boy waved it front of the leather jock strap 'Him understand this.'

Very slowly the green boy unhooked his strap from the side and took it off. His cock sprang out pulsing and a slow drop of pink fluid squeezed out

'Him flucky ten hours belly slow belly good . . . You want black fruit? cost fifty dollar for you him me and one nice girl'

'all right.'

'you show money.'

Jerry took out a fifty dollar bill . . . the boy hummed 'a fifty dollar bill and then . . . come along Johnny.'

They started down the railroad which was overgrown with weeds. The lizard boy walked on all fours gripping the rusty track. The railroad had been built on a ridge of limestone surrounded on all sides by stagnant streams and swamps to the sky. The black boy pointed to a bank of phosphorescent clouds on the West horizon 'Phosphor storm . . . plenty bad . . . burn Melican tourists . . . !' He made a shrinking curling gesture with one black hand. The boy passed a hand over his face and looked around with helpless stupidity 'Mother what is it? Before him wake up he fried potatoes ... patatas fritas ...'

They walked down limestone steps and followed a path along a stream to a bridge which led them to a little island. Jerry saw several thatch huts. In the middle of the island was a small pavilion open at the side. The floor was paved with limestone and there was a row of seats with holes in the middle like toilet seats facing each other. The seats were polished smooth and yellow with use and under them indentations had been worn by twisting feet. A ladder of polished wood leaned against a lattice work partition.

'Me go now bring black fruit nice girl.' he pointed to the green boy 'his sister'.

Jerry walked over and looked at the green water green lizard boy you got money with slow idiot smile take off leather sleeping Johnny cost fifty dollar for you black fruit island plenty good spasms unbuttoned his meester so what muttering slow lizard people so what hunger in his stomach so come along Johnny on all fours.

'Come along Johnny black fruit ready.'

Leather pallets spread on the floor on a large leaf four phosphorescent black fruit. The boy's sister a green shade he could see the lattice work through her body.

The black boy held out a leather jock strap 'Put that on Johnny.'

Jerry blushed muttering 'all right' and started to unbutton his shirt feeling the blood rush to his crotch well so what he thought kicked off his sandals dropped his pants and shorts stood there naked his whole body blushing.

The black boy pushed Jerry's penis down between his legs and adjusted the jock strap with gentle mocking fingers.

'Johnny fuck leather now.'

They sat down on the pallets and the boy passed him a black fruit. The sweet rotten taste ached through his body.

'Fruit act soon now. You see.'

The lizard pair unhooked their jock straps and the black boy unhooked Jerry's strap. They sat down on the toilet seats opposite each other sweet rotten smell soft mucilagenous fingers caressing his prostate inside bubbling all the dirty words. He shivered and kicked and whimpered goose pimples swept over his body a hot shit and all process together feeling the fruit his soft fingers could have been Ohio the dirty words shivered over his body ruined toilet a nice afternoon no hurry what you want plenty slow.

'Secretary of State for Ruined Toilet God damn it what you trying to sell here Farmer Brown?'

When they all come together he blacks out sweet and rotten its this nerve gas they got Gertie you lose control over all your physical processes they were shoving him up the ladder some one kissed a noose around his neck silver light popped in his eyes guide know meesters in a decent hotel licking each other stroking his limestones unbutton his meester so what he thought kicking slow lizard peoples well so what he thought kicking to the sky hunger know meester Johnny up ladder . . .

He was lying there on the floor of the pavilion tried to get up paralyzed neck must be broken tried to turn his head light popped in his eyes again an aching pain down the spine to the groin spurts across his stomach . . .

Technical Sergeant Brady from Camouflage on leave and off limits 'You want nice girl mister?' a boy standing there naked except for red underwear shorts thin red haired kid with freckles. Brady can do with a piece of ass but a feller has to be careful off limits man eating whores out here and the black fruit . . . Brady had read the bulletins the Captain's voice in his ear . . . 'If you fellers do go off limits for God's sake remember this is another planet you're a long long way from Columbus Ohio.'

They were walking down a path by a stream could have been Ohio except the oaks weren't exactly oaks good copy though a dead leaf fell on the boy's shoulder got their seasons mixed too a bull head surfaced ostentatiously in the stream nice afternoon no hurry about the piece of ass might turn out a 'Purple People Eater' remember the bulletins the Captains voice in his ear . . . 'If she starts to turn purple, boys, and spread out at the edges grab your pants and split while you got what pants should cover.'

Any case he could pick his ass remembering what chocolate bought in Italy remembering all the wars that's what the front is like in this war all the old war films those mad queens from Camouflage flouncing about in Vietnam drag looking for a piece of ass indeed get her . . . They sit on a bench by the stream. Brady gives the kid some chocolate the boy smearing his face with it kicks his legs out and giggles. Brady can see the kid has a hard on puts his arms around the kid's shoulders. The kid slips his shorts down leaning forward kicks them in the grass by the stream wriggles up on Brady's lap and says 'Jack me off Mister' chocolate on his breath in Brady's ear arched his body when he came spurts across his stomach fading smell of semen in the still afternoon air poses a colorless question . . . Is the boy there?

Green lizard boy stands on the bank of a stagnant stream by the weed grown railroad. He rubs his worn leather jock strap with a slow smile.

'You come with me Meester?'

streets of idiot pleasure youth memory ghost spasm slow linen to the floor under the strong brown hands street boy faces jade flutes tapping spine centers . . . Green flares burst our heads. His body shot from spine and the strong brown hands were mine

'Me thing like jelly fish Meester.'

liquifying gook over your body of pink honey blue cocoon crystals froze the larval flesh . . . street boys of the green with cruel idiot smiles aromatic jasmine excrement pubic hairs that cut needles of pleasure through the diseased flesh

'You win something like jelly fish Meester.'

clear green face smile of idiot death spasms a smell of slow animal ferment and vegetable decay filmed his amber flesh cysted with bright lizards and beetles sweet diarrhoea smells young hard ons of flower flesh breath of rotten crab people always there when the egg cracks and white juice spurts from ruptured spines

'This bad place Meester. This place of last fuck for Johnny' – tapping spine –

from his mouth floated coal gas and violets . . . on the boy's breath a flesh . . . The boy dropped his rusty black pants a delicate must film of soiled linen over the brown flesh in the blue walled room kief and mint tea clothes stiff with oil on the red tiled floor naked and sullen street boy senses darted around the room for scraps of advantage . . . smell of rain on horse flesh and dust of cities black vomit of Panama spectral lust of school toilets

'You come with me to jack off in 1929 Mister?'

the hard brown hands and his body slid from spine in yellow light vegetable switch to the drenched lands coated jasmine excrement winding pleasure labyrinths of intestinal street boys stranger color through his eyes the look out different

'*Who* look out different? Quien es?'

hard on spreading nutty smell through the outhouse bone spasms in cocaine ass green mirrors moving the boy's flesh when the pink egg cracks bed bug smell of rose wall paper

'Me thing like green lizard. sweet boy on the bank Meester.'

tasting cutting face transparent with all the sewers of death black fruit orgasm aromatic sweet rot on ditto flesh vegetable pleasure boys pop spine

'Slow fruit and this the jelly . . . one black spasm in bad place Meester.' The boy dropped rusty black flesh and dust of cities cooking paregoric black vomit linen yellow fever of Panama barracks steaming rain smell under the iron roof stale clothes metal sullen animal eyes hair plates of black pleasure aromatic flower flesh leaking alternate terminal flesh when the rose egg cracks

'Last flucky you come with me Meester.'

faded Panama photo soiled linen under the ceiling fan lust of shuttered rooms . . . tents haunted by masturbating boys the upland pond soaked in clouds shivering evenings scraps of advantage over flop house flesh naked sullen street boy outhouse of cities must film of barracks jissom clothes heavy and stiff in neetles . . . The boy tapped his rusty code on rose wall paper . . . sound of vibrated rectal tubes black vomit yellowed in faded Panama pants flags clatter in the afternoon wind barrack steam shivering excrement and rain smells mirror of masturbating afternoons ejaculates wet dreams through stale Weimar youth post card fjords dead rainbow flesh

Unit I White: room in Northern hotel . . . pilots on leave . . . Luftwaffe uniforms . . . Lugers on hotel chairs . . . timeless young faces invaded by steel and oil . . . 'ich will dick ins bauch fickeln' . . . melting naked identical erections rubbing blond pubic hairs

Unit II Black: Black Genuau dancer beating drum rhythms on the boy's diaphragm whirling and twisting the boy to the pounding drums

Unit III Green: vaseline on finger . . . smells of oil and metal . . . 'loosen you up a bit' . . . rubs jelly in the green brown rectal flesh with a low circular pull . . . ass hairs spread over the tide flats

Unit IV Red: red haired boy . . . smoky rose sun set . . . room with rose wall paper . . . 'here goes' . . . blood sang and pounded in his eyes and ears

Unit V Blue: orgasms puff white smoke across a blue sky cut by vapor trails . . . The units permutate 2 1 3 4 5 Unit II Black: hands beating drum rhythms on his chest and diaphragm bent over the hotel chair . . . Unit I White: hard bodies alert from image ray war cool mist drifting in the northern room follows hand down spine to spread ass cheeks . . . Unit III Green twisting finger in

rectum turns to vine tendril ... green uniforms on the chair ...
Unit IV Red: drop of pearly lubricant in pink light ... iron mesas
lit by a pink volcano ... 'here goes' choking in a red mist ... Unit
V Blue: fading train whistles blue winds of silence blue sky bluer
and bluer before the splintering purple crash ... The Units
permutate 3 2 1 4 5: 'to spread ass cheeks you wanta Unit III'
Green ... He squeezes finger in rectum turns oil and metal ...
blossom green uniforms on green brown flesh ... sighs with the
finger pull: 'loosen you up a bit. Bend over.' ... Unit II Black:
drapes himself to the drum ... the black hotel chair touches his
stomach ... Unit I White: young faces melting naked from the
image ray back to spread ass cheeks ... snow slope under the
northern shirt ... Unit IV Red: 'Here goes' red leg hairs rubbing
rose wall paper phantom whirlpools of masturbation out in drifting
snow dust smoke and dead leaves word dust drifting 'I wanta
screw you' 'Bend over' 'Loosen your ass a bit' 'here goes' slow
spread smoke finger in rectum old photos turning a slow whirl of
word dust masturbating ghost rectums a sea of legs and sex hairs
shifting spiral of phantoms ... 'Bend over you' 'Spread' 'Breathe
in. Here goes' 'Over' stirring a slow rectum gate ... whirlpools of
light slow down to statues in a deserted Northern park

It was a red brick house on a cliff by the river brown yellow wall
paper peeling from the plaster pieces of plaster crunch under my
feet brown stains on the ceiling of the front room. It does look as if
the roof leaks. Under the stairs I find an old diary which seems to
consist largely of household accounts here and there almost illegible
references to the rooms upstairs which I gather were rented out at
one time. This reminds me that I have not yet been upstairs. I go
to the foot of the stairs and remember the leaking faucet. Perhaps
I should check. Yes the washer I put in is still holding – (Fixed his
faucet you didn't? he was getting old in any case) – So back to the
stairs when it occurs to me that I should check the grounds first.
At this point I realize that some force is trying to prevent me from
going upstairs and I determine to do so at once. There is a knock
at the side door. I go down the steep wooden stairs and open the
door. Three boys are standing there in old cut clothes. One of the
boys steps forward and says

'You go upstairs with me Mister?'

The other two boys standing there with their arms around each
other's shoulders giggle and whisper something

'I know downstairs upstairs basement. Live down there.' He gestured towards the river. 'This bad house you buy Mister.'

I decided that the boys might be helpful in finding workmen to redecorate and invited them in. They followed me up the wooden stairs to the front room giggling

'Now we go upstairs Mister' said the boy who had spoken first. The other two boys stayed in what had once been the drawing room. I started up the stairs the boy behind me. The house seemed to get older as if I was walking up through phantom years and stale memories – ('These stairs . . . They'll be the death of me . . .' Memory hit the old detective like a knife 'God! Now I remember! room 18 on the top floor . . .') – We stood now in a dusty hall opening on three rooms that had evidently been built in a large attic. The rooms had been partitioned off and covered over. Above them stretched the beams and roof of the house

'This room 18'

The room opposite the stairwell bore the number 18 crudely drawn in black paint. The door was locked. I brought out a ring of keys that the estate agent had given me. The boy took the key ring from my hand and opened the door. The window was boarded up the room dank and musty. Rose wall paper clung to the plaster in patches. There was a brass bed springs rusted through the mattress a black wardrobe with a pivot mirror a wash stand by the window had been disconnected rusty pipes exposed. I stood in front of the mirror trying to picture the tenant who had lived here long ago. The boy came and stood by my elbow. I had jumped it would seem at his touch as if the absent tenant had laid a slow cold hand on my shoulder

'Boy who used to live here like this.' The boy put a hand on his hip and minced over to the wash stand. He went through a pantomime of fixing his hair. He turned from the washstand and walked to the closet. 'Hang self here.' He opened the closet door. The ceiling did not cover the closet. Looking up I could see beams under the roof. The boy stuck out his tongue and lolled his head on one side. He brought his arm up from the elbow and sniggered – (little snigger in the dark room remember?) –

'And the other rooms?'

'Come along Mister. I show you. Know this house . . . plenty bad place. You see.'

He led the way down the hall. 'This room 23' 23 in red paint. At first glance no 23 seemed much like no 18 . . . patches of wall paper in red and green patterns that affected me unpleasantly white enamel bed stand flaked off to rusty iron. The wall above the bed was charred and a few remnants of the charred mattress clung to black bed springs

'Man who live here drink much' the boy made a gesture 'Take pills.' He swallowed a handful of phantom pills. 'One night mattress catch fire. He wake up everything burned off from here down.' The boy put his hand just below the belt. 'This' he touched his genitals 'burned off. Legs like that' He gestured to the blackened springs. 'He died at once?'

The boy shook his head. 'Three days screaming. The scream when he first wake up I hear it down there.' He gestured towards the river. We were in front of the third door . . . 16 in sepia.

'What happened to 16?'

The boy looked at me with a closed expression 'I don't know. We see now.'

From within the room I could hear voices and laughing. 'Why there is some one in there'

'My two friends'

'What are they doing?'

The boy shrugged 'Having fun with each other I guess.' He opened the door. Room 16 seemed in much better repair than the other two blue wall paper with ship scenes faded yellow curtains at the window. The wash stand was connected and spattered with fresh urine. I turned and looked at the bed. The two boys there naked were kissing in a strange animal fashion with teeth bared. They seemed unaware of our presence. One of the boys had urinated in front of the third door. I turned and looked at the sepia bed. The boy naked touched his gentials teeth bared

'They off my two friends'

Having fun in front of the third boy. Now one boy had mounted the other on all fours. The boys turned into dogs and made whimpering noises that stirred in my throat – (slow cold whispers in my throat and the words were mine once) – The boy flicked my shirt 'Take off your clothes Mister it's getting late. Not much time left.'

He hung his shirt over the wardrobe mirror. He kicked off his shoes and dropped his pants and shorts.

'Whee Mister' He made a gesture of a plane flying upwards at a steep angle. I had followed his movements and stood there naked but who was 'I'? a thin boy looked like me. Sad young image steps from the film dripping dew . . . the boy solid I could touch almost

'You come with me to jack off in 1920 movie?'

whimpering noises teeth bared drops spattered . . . bubbles of orange light in the room . . . from a great distance I could see the boys . . . a thin boy looked like me . . . sperm on the mattress . . . boy's belt . . . I could touch . . .

'You almost there. Come with me to a movie. Whee Mister bubbles of light!'

blue wall paper washing around bare feet peanut shells on the floor . . . from a great distance boy's belt . . . a thin boy putting on his clothes now running down the stairs . . . very cold here and always darker . . . boys running towards the cliff . . . one boy turns and waves to the house . . . the boy I was hand lifted . . . he could climb down the cliff . . .

'Look out! Be careful!'

without a throat without a tongue seeing the ledge that would crumble . . . boy falling . . . weeds and bushes spatter his face with dew . . . base of the cliff one leg twisted under him boy I was who never would be now further and further away a speck of white that seemed to catch all the light left on a dying star and suddenly I lost him . . . a great distance . . . it was cold here and would be now darker . . . boys further and running further away . . . the cliff . . . the boy . . . a speck of quick white that seemed to show all others how the light left a dying star . . . down the cliff I lost him . . . the boy falling . . . weeds and bushes . . . dew spatters my film from a great distance . . . the light left a darker star . . . deep and blue the cliff . . . I lost him long ago . . . dying there . . . light went out . . . my film ends . . .

'I want *Central Heating*! sex in clothes American rain outside! If you young fellers on the golf course yahu one more Montana tape tent child sex in a bedroll – they smell to California out through the idiot sun set at 23 Panhandle Door! Might be just what I am look . . . old fairy without a sun . . . I am the Director . . . You have known me for a long time . . . Mister, leave cigarette money . . .'

13

WHERE YOU BELONG

My trouble began when they decide I am executive timber – It starts like this: a big blond driller from Dallas picks me out of the labor pool to be his houseboy in a prefabricated air-conditioned bungalow – He comes on rugged but as soon as we strip down to the ball park over on his stomach kicking white wash and screams out 'Fuck the shit out of me!' – I give him a slow pimp screwing and in solid – When this friend comes down from New York the driller says 'This is the boy I was telling you about' – and friend looks me over slow chewing his cigar and says: 'What are you doing over there with the apes? Why don't you come over here with the Board where you belong?' And he slips me a long slimy look friend works for the Trak News Agency – 'We don't report the news – We write it.' And next thing I know they have trapped a grey flannel suit on me and I am sent to this school in Washington to learn how this writing the news before it happens is done – I sus it is the Mayan caper with an IBM machine and I don't want to be caught short in a grey flannel suit when the lid blows off – So I act in concert with the Subliminal Kid who is a technical sergeant and has a special way of talking. And he stands there a long time chewing tobacco is our middle name – What are you doing over there? – Beat your mother to over here – Know what they mean if they start job for instance? – Open shirt, apparent sensory impressions calling slimy terms of old fifty fifty jazz – Kiss their target all over – assembly points in Danny Deaver – by now they are controlling shit house of the world – just feed in sad-eyed youths and the machine will process it – after that Minraud sky – their eggs all over – These officers come gibbering into the queer bar don't even know what buttons to push – ('Run with the apes? Why don't you come across the lawn?') And he gives me a long slimy responsible cum grey flannel suit and I am Danny Deaver in drag writing 'the news is served, sir.' Hooded dead gibber: 'this is the Mayan Caper' – a fat cigar and a long white nightie – Non-payment answer is simple as Board Room Reports rigged a thousand years – Set up excuse and the machine will process it – Mouldy pawn ticket runs a thousand years chewing the same argument – I Sekuin perfected that art along the Tang Dynasty – To put it another way IBM machine controls thought feeling and *apparent* sensory impressions – subliminal lark – These officers don't even know what buttons to push – Whatever you feed into the machine on subliminal level the machine will process – So we feed in 'dismantle thyself' and authority emaciated down to answer Mr Of The Account in Ewyork, Onolulu, Aris, Ome, Oston – Might be just what I am look' –

We fold writers of all time in together and record radio programs, movie sound-tracks, TV and juke box songs all the words of the world stirring around in a cement mixer and pour in the resistance message 'Calling partisans of all nations – Cut word lines – Shift linguals – Free doorways – Vibrate "tourists" – Word falling – Photo falling – Break through in Grey Room'

So the District Supervisor calls me in and puts the old white schmaltz down on me:

'Now kid what are you doing over there with the niggers and the apes? Why don't you straighten out and act like a white man? – After all they're only human cattle – You know that yourself – Hate to see a bright young man fuck up and get off on the wrong track – Sure it happens to all of us one time or another – Why the man who went on to invent Shitola was sitting right where you're sitting now twenty-five years ago and I was saying the same things to him – Well he straightened out the way you're going to straighten out – Yes sir that Shitola combined with an ape diet – All we have to do is press the button and a hundred million more or less gooks flush down the drain in green cancer piss – That's *big* isn't it? – And any man with white blood in him wants to be part of something big – You can't deny your blood kid – You're *white white white* – And you can't walk out on Trak – There's just no place to go.'

Most distasteful thing I ever stood still for – enough to make a girl crack her calories – So I walk out and the lid blew off –

14

URANIAN WILLY

Uranian Willy the Heavy Metal Kid, also known as Willy The Rat – He wised up the marks.

'This is war to extermination – Fight cell by cell through bodies and mind screens of the earth – souls rotten from the Orgasm Drug – Flesh shuddering from the Ovens – prisoners of the earth, come out – Storm the studio'.

His plan called for total exposure – Wise up all the marks everywhere show them the rigged wheel – Storm the Reality Studio and retake the universe – The plan shifted and reformed as reports came in from his electric patrols sniffing quivering down streets of the earth – the Reality Film giving and buckling like a bulk head under pressure – burnt metal smell of interplanetary war in the raw noon streets swept by screaming glass blizzards of enemy flak.

'Photo falling – Word falling – Use partisans of all nation – Target Orgasm Ray Installations – Gothenberg Sweden – Coordinates 8 2 7 6 – Take Studio – Take Board Books – Take Death Dwarfs – Towers, open fire.'

Pilot K9 caught the syndicate killer image on a penny arcade screen and held it in his sight – Now he was behind it in it was it – The image disintegrated in photo flash of total recognition – other image on screen – Hold in sight – smell of burning metal in his head – 'Pilot K9, you are cut off – Back – Back – Back before the whole fucking shit house goes up – Return to base immediately – Ride music beam back to base – Stay out of that time Flak – All pilots ride Pan Pipes back to base.'

It was impossible to estimate the damage – Board books destroyed – Enemy personnel decimated – The message of total resistance on short wave of the world.

'Calling partisans of all nation – Shift linguals – Cut word lines – Vibrate tourists – Free doorways – Photo falling – Word falling – Break through in Grey Room.'

White Street ... noon ticker tape ... plea ray explodes ... zero eaten by crab ... Carl broke through in grey room ... recorder twisting approval ray ... switchboard screens: zero eaten by crab ... word falling ... night set explodes in White St ... high fi the area ... crab word falling ... break through in grey room ...

Carl passed through a barrier of dust in a grey room filled with funeral urns the recorder twisting a slow word dust dirtied his body falling through space between worlds

Border City ... noon ticker tape ... word falling ... the board flakes of electricals* ... break through in grey room ... photo falling ... down into present time and there investigate purpose ... distant city is Red Mesa ... fight erupt like sand on iron ... sacrifice partisans and rioters of all nations ... gambling fight ... attack at arbitrary intervals ... investigate purpose ... sacrifice partisans of all nations ... open fire on priest shriek for humans ... he never mesh with Iron Claws ... investigate distant city ...

Garden priests shriek: 'Die Jungle and Flowers bouncing they can't city?'

'Thing connections!'

'Chemical gardens in rusty shit peoples!'

'The city can also be a fat starting gate.'

'Tengo, vea stopping starting gate cones!'

'Soy Time! Tengo connectiones!'

P.M. ticker tape wires gambling foe of the city ... he void cut like sand pens ... streets with flame gates ... thing connections void ... sacrifice partisans ... sacrifice Iron Claws ... connections cut in blue sights of the whistling priest ...

* note on 'electricals': The weapon of invasion is precisely *alternating current* yes no stop go at the rate of sixty shifts per second of the sound and image track. Here is a simple example 'Come on in and have a drink, friend' friendly smile outstretched hand.

'Drink your drink and get out you fucking fruit!' ugly American snarl hand pointing to the door.

Now alternate the two sound and image tracks sixty alternation per second until the man smiles from the other side face fuzzing out of focus pieces of smile and snarl hanging in the air like clusters of white hot wire. These creatures made from alternating sound and image track are known as 'electricals.'

15

GONGS OF VIOLENCE

The war between the sexes split the planet into armed camps right down the middle line divides one thing from the other – And I have seen them all: The lesbian colonels in tight green uniforms, the young aides and directives regarding the Sex Enemy from proliferating departments.

On the line is the baby and semen market where the sexes meet to exchange the basic commodity which is known as 'the property' – unborn properties are shown with a time projector. As a clear young going face flashes on the auction screen frantic queens of all nations screem: 'A doll! A doll! A doll!' And tear each other to pieces with leopard claws and broken bottles – tobacco auction sound-effects – Riots erupt like sandstorms spraying the market with severed limbs and bouncing heads.

Biological parents in most cases are not owners of 'the property'. They act under orders of absentee proprietors to install the indicated stops that punctuate the written life script – With each 'property' goes a life script – Shuttling between property farmers and script writers, a legion of runners, fixers, guides, agents, brokers, faces insane with purpose, mistakes and confusion pandemic – Like a buyer has a first class 'property' and a lousy grade B life script

'Fuck my life script will you you cheap down grade bitch!'

Everywhere claim-jumpers and time-nappers jerk the time position of a 'property'

'And left me standing there without a "spare jacket" or a "greyhound" to travel in, my "property" back in 1910 Panama – I don't even feel like a human without my "property" – How can I feel without fingers?'

'The property' can also be jerked forward in time and sold at any age – the life of advanced 'property' is difficult to say the least: poison virus agents trooping in and out at all hours: 'We just dropped in to see some friends a population of patrols' – Strangers from Peoria waving quit claim deeds, skip tracers, collectors, claim jumpers demanding payment for alleged services say: 'We own the other half of "the property".'

'I dunno, me – Only work here – Technical sergeant.'

'Have you seen Slotless City?'

Red mesas cut by time winds – a network of bridges, ladders, catwalks, cable cars, escalators and ferris wheels down into the blue depths – The precarious occupants in this place without phantom guards live in iron cubicles – constant motion on tracks, gates click open shut – buzzes, blue sparks, and constant breakage – (Whole squares and tiers of the city plunge into the bottomless void) – swinging beams of construction and blue flares on the calm intent young worker faces – People rain on the city in homemade gliders and rockets – Balloons drift down out of faded violet photos – The city is reached overland by a series of trails cut in stone, suspension bridges and ladders intricately booby-trapped, wrong maps, disappearing guides – (A falling bureaucrat in blue glasses screams by with a flash of tin: 'Soy de la policia, senores – Tengo connectiones') hammocks, swings, balconies over the void – chemical gardens in rusty troughs – Flowers and seeds and mist settle down from high jungle above the city – Fights erupt like sand storms, through iron streets a wake of shattered bodies, heads bouncing into the void, hands clutching bank notes from gambling fights – Priests shriek for human sacrifices, gather partisans to initiate unspeakable rites until they are destroyed by counter pressures – Vigilantes of every purpose hang anyone they can overpower – Workers attack the passerby with torches and air hammers – They reach up out of manholes and drag the walkers down with iron claws – Rioters of all nations storm the city in a landslide of flame-throwers and Molotov cocktails – Sentries posted everywhere in towers open fire on the crowds at arbitrary intervals – The police never mesh with present time, their investigation far removed from the city always before or after the fact erupt into any cafe and machine gun the patrons – The city pulses with slotless purpose lunatics killing from behind the wall of glass – A moment's hesitation brings a swarm of con men, guides, whores, mooches, script writers, runners, fixers cruising and snapping like aroused sharks –

(The subway sweeps by with a black blast of iron.)

The Market is guarded by Mongolian Archers right in the middle line between sex pressures jetting a hate wave that disintegrates violators in a flash of light – Everywhere posted on walls and towers in hovering autogyros these awful archers only get relief from the pressure by blasting a violator – Screen eyes vibrate through the city like electric dogs sniffing for violations

Remind the Board of the unsavory case of 'Black Paul' who bought babies with centipede jissom – When the fraud came to light a whole centipede issue was in the public streets and every citizen went armed with a flame-thrower – So the case of Black Paul shows what happens when all sense of civic responsibility breaks down –

It was a transitional period because of the Synthetics and everybody was raising some kinda awful life form in his bidet to fight the Sex Enemy – The results were not in all respects reasonable men, but the Synthetics were rolling off that line and we were getting some damned interesting types by golly blue heavy metal boys with near zero metabolism that shit once a century and then it's a slag heap and disposal problem in the worst form there is: sewage delta to a painted sky under orange gas flares, islands of garbage where green boy-girls tend human heads in chemical gardens, terminal cities under the metal word fallout like cold melted solder on walls and streets, sputtering cripples with phorphorescent metal stumps – So we decided the blue heavy metal boys were not in all respects a good blueprint.

I have seen them all – A unit yet of mammals and vegetables that subsist each on the shit of the other in predestiginal symbiosis and achieved a stage where one group shit out nothing but pure carbon dioxide which the other unit breathed in to shit out oxygen – It's the only way to live – You understand they had this highly developed culture with life forms between insect and vegetable, hanging vines, stinging sex hairs – The whole deal was finally relegated to It-Never-Happened-Department.

'Retroactive amnesia it out of every fucking mind screen in the area if we have to – How long you want to bat this tired old act around? A centipede issue in the street, unusual beings dormant in cancer, hierarchical shit-eating units – Now by all your stupid Gods at once let's not get this show on the road let's stop it.'

Posted everywhere on street corners the idiot irresponsibles twitter supersonic approval, repeating slogans, giggling, dancing, masturbating out windows, making machine-guns-noises and police whistles 'And you, Dead Hand, stretching the Vegetable People come out of that compost heap – You are not taking your old fibrous roots past this inspector'.

And the idiot irresponsibles scream posted everywhere in chorus: 'Chemical gardens in rusty shit peoples!!'

'All out of time and into space. Come out of the time-word "the" forever. Come out of the body word "thee" forever. There is nothing to fear. There is no thing in space. There is no word to fear. There is no word in space.'

And the idiot irresponsibles scream: 'Come out of your stupid body you nameless assholes!!'

And there were those who thought A.J. lost dignity through the idiotic behavior of these properties but He said:

'That's the way I like to see them. No fallout. What good ever came from thinking? Just look there' (another heavy metal boy sank through the earth's crust and we got some good pictures . . .) 'one of Shaffer's blueprints. I sounded a word of warning.'

His idiot irresponsibles twittered and giggled and masturbated over him from little swings and snapped bits of food from his plate screaming: 'Blue people NG conditions! Typical sight leak out!'

'All out of time and into space.'

'Hello, Ima Johnny. the naked astronaut.'

And the idiot irresponsibles rush in with space-suits and masturbating rockets spatter the city with jissom.

'Do not be alarmed citizens of Annexia – Report to your Nearie Pro Station for Chlorophyll Processing – We are converting to Vegetable State – Emergency measure to counter the Heavy Metal Peril – Go to you "Nearie" – You will meet a cool, competent person who will dope out all your fears in photosynthesis – Calling all citizens of Annexia – Report to Green Sign for Processing.'

'Citizens of Gravity we are converting all out to Heavy Metal. Carbonic Plague of the Vegetable People threatens our Heavy Metal State. Report to your nearest Plating Station. It's fun to be plated,' says this well-known radio and TV personality who is now engraved forever in gags of metal. 'Do not believe the calumny that our metal fallout will turn the planet into a slag heap. And in any case, is that worse than a compost heap? heavy Metal is our program and we are prepared to sink through it . . .'

The cold heavy fluid settled in his spine 70 tons per square inch – cool blocks of SOS – (Solid Blue Silence) – under heavy time – Can anything be done to Metal People of Uranus? – heavy his answer in monotone disaster stock: 'Nobody can kick an SOS habit – 70 tons per square inch – the crust from the beginning you understand – Tortured Metal Oz of earthquakes is tons focus of this junk – sudden young energy – I got up and danced – know eventually be relieved – That's all I need – I got up and danced the disasters – '

Gongs of violence and how – Show you something – berserk machine – 'Shift cut tangle word lines – Word falling – Photo falling – '

'I said The Chief of Police skinned alive in Baghdad not Washington D.C.'

'Switzerland freezes all foreign assets.'

'*Foreign assets?*'

'What? – British Prime Minister assassinated in Rightist coup?'

'Mindless idiot you have liquidated the Commissar.'

'Terminal electric voice of C – All ling door out of agitated – Ta ta Stalin – Carriage age ta – '

Spectators scream through the track – The electronic brain shivers in blue and pink and chlorophyll orgasms spitting out money printed on rolls of toilet paper, condoms full of ice cream, Kotex hamburgers – Police files of the world spurt out in a blast of bone meal, garden tools and barbecue sets whistle through the air, skewer the spectators – crumpled cloth bodies through dead nitrous streets of an old film set – Grey luminous flakes falling softly on Ework, Onolulu, Aris, Ome, Oston – from siren towers the twanging tones of fear – Pan God of Panic piping blue notes through empty streets as the berserk time machine twisted a tornado of years and centuries – wind through dusty offices and archives – Board Books scattered to rubbish heaps of the earth – symbol books of the all-powerful board that had controlled thought feeling and movement of a planet from birth to death with iron claws of pain and pleasure – The whole structure of reality went up in silent explosions – paper moon and muslin trees and in the black silver sky great rents as the cover of the world rained down –

Biologic film went up ... raining dinosaurs 'It sometimes happens ... just an old showman' Death takes over the game so many actors buildings and stars laid flat pieces of finance over the golf course summer afternoons bare feet waiting for rain smell of sickness in the room Switzerland Panama machine guns in Baghdad rising from the typewriter pieces of finance on the evening wind tin shares Buenos Aires Mr. Martin smiles old names waiting sad old tune haunted the last human attic.

Outside a 1920 movie theatre in East St. Louis I met Johnny

Yen – His face showed strata of healed and half-healed fight scars – Standing there under the luminous film flakes he said: 'I am going to look for a room in a good neighborhood' –

Captain Clark welcomes you aboard this languid paradise of dreamy skies and firefly evenings music across the golf course echos from high cool corners of the dining room a little breeze stirs candles on the table. Its was an April afternoon. After a while some news boy told him the war was over sadness in his eyes trees filtering light on dappled grass the lake like bits of silver paper in a wind across the golf course fading streets a distant sky

Lee took the bus over a long viaduct to reach the island of Land's Wadt. The bus was sixty feet long with an intricate arrangement of seats and swings on various levels. The bus had been standing still for a long time. Customs officials moved through the bus stopping to nod out and munch fruit with boneless gums.

Lee grabbed a spastic's crutch and charged the passport line screaming 'I'm going centipede.' Stamp it quick. 'No good conditions. Typical sights leak out.'

The customs official held Lee's passport and looked at it from hooded eyes swaying back and forth his knees folding slightly. He put the passport against a partition leaned his weight on the seal and nodded out. Lee rocked him back gently and stepped down into a dusty warehouse. Shadowy grey figures stood about spitting munching fruit and talking a sort of primitive English with hiatuses and oblique time switches the words hanging in the air like winter breath. Lee noticed that everything was covered with a soft grey metal like cold melted solder slow word fall out. He walked through a vacant lot and checked into a red brick hotel. While he was washing there was a muffled knock and a boy entered muttering unknown names. The boy had a smooth yellow face and brown eyes that caught points of light in the dim hotel room

'It's dangerous you dig like I have to get this Rx. I know a croaker might write'

muttering face and brown eyes that stood around hotel room talking primitive English with hiatuses

'And it's dangerous you dig lie word hanging in air like croaker might write'

'Wait here' said the boy 'I don't want him to rumble you. This old croaker sometimes his motor centers give out and he can't move but if you catch him at the right intersection he's an automatic obedient. And he doesn't know who's talking anyhoo who does?'

Lee waited in a deserted lunch counter the tables and chairs covered with grey paste and walked the empty streets under a soft steady rain of metal word fall out.

'He wrote finally. I had to fuck his old lady with a strap on the horrible old cunt digest the rubber'

The druggist started back with a cry of rage; 'Oh no!'

'We don't do that kind of business.'

'What are you the doctor?'

'Do yourself one favor and beat it.'

'We don't handle it' she said pointedly looking at the boy's fly. Filled it finally in Wallgreen's 'You gotta be careful with this stuff, a little too much and you can call the red wagon'

Lee watched the drug shoot through Johnny's body like puffs of blue smoke. The room was empty with white tile floors and walls. In the center of the room under neon runes was an elaborate plastic frame sphere shaped attached to the floor with plastic cups. Johnny zipped off his clothes walking rhythmically around the room dropping a piece here and a piece there stood naked with a bottle of Coca-Cola . . . 'Don't be alone out there' he hummed softly flicking light switches with his feet They sat down on the frame which adjusted to their naked buttocks touching the rectums. Johnny handed a jar of unguent to Lee. 'Here use this.' Johnny draped himself over the frame and Lee adjusted his body stretching a knee here an elbow there and wherever he pushed Johnny's limbs in the frame they stuck like rubber . . . Lee opened the jar which was filled with a substance like frog eggs little black specks imbedded in greenish jelly. Lee spread the jelly over Johnny's body suspended in a crystal web . . . The boy's flesh dissolved in the unguent losing outlines fuzzing out in blue light . . . Lee straddled the boy's body one shuddering white flash the bodies lit up inside pulsing bluer and bluer incandescent purple blue flash back the two young bodies stuck together like dogs sharp white teeth shine through parted lips . . . boy brown eyes and yellow hair . . . the boy was dressing in front of a stainless steel locker

The druggist started back: 'Don't be alone out there', he hummed.

'Oh no.'

'We don't want that kind of naked buttocks touching.'

'What are you the doctor of unguent?'

'Here use this.'

See here an elbow and there and wherever fly the frame they

116

stuck there like filled it finally the jar which was filled with a stuff with little black specks Lee watched the drug of rotten protoplasm contracted his tubes. The flesh dissolved over Johnny's body suspended spurts of blue jelly like flesh were dissolving in the unguent one pulsing blue in white light Lee watching from cold blue center. In his brain the quivering sphere shaped to blue in a crystal web. Johnny stripped off his blue boy the room the stainless steel locker ... softly flickering light frames which adjusted business ... the rectums Johnny draped himself over his body stretching. He pushed Johnny's limbs catatonic rubber spread the pulsing blue light inside him a crystal web. The boys puffed blue smoke two bodies fuzzing the web one shuddering white tile walls in polar distance blue haloes flickering ... a pulsing blue sphere over skeletons locked in limestone.

16

DEAD FINGERS TALK

The boy from the North came to the Rock on a cold Spring wind through courtyards and cubicles opening on balconies connected by ladders, catwalks iron bridges – wind of metal through the boy from the North with the blue sickness of opium in his bones and the heavy mineral affinities in his cool blue eyes cloud mines and mills and oil derricks stretching iron claws of monopoly – The Master almost gave the order to remove the boy from the reservation – Then a move appeared on his chess board of agents and the order to remove the boy was canceled –

'Yes, Mr. Bradly Mr. Martin, a chess move – i Sabbah set Bradly in the door.'

Move the boy from the North to Tangier present time – He walked on grey silent as a fish through shadow pools and doorways – Here comes a guide from the Blue Movies – Scatter on grey into dark windows old gangster films and news reels fading in 'Smoke Domino Cigarettes' – dead neon in the noon sun – The guide did not see me – spinning fractured light down all your streets and by the river junk sick in dawn mist took the ferry from Algiers to New Orleans – grey powder in spoons shaking junk sick hands – over the grey subway down Cook Street – sliding between light and shadow – Word falling – photo falling – break through in Grey Room – agent of Hassan i Sabbah along newsprint

WAS WEIGHTLESS – NEW YORK HERALD TRIBUNE PARIS APRIL 17, 1961 – 'One's arms and legs in and out through the crowd weigh nothing – grey dust of broom in old cabin – Mr. Bradly Mr. I Myself sit in the chair as i subways and basements did before that – but hung in dust and pain wind – My hand writing leaning to a boy's grey flannel pants did not change although vapor trails fading in hand does not weigh anything now – Gagarin said grey junk yesterdays trailing the earth was quite plain and past the American he could easily see the shores of continents – islands and great rivers.'

Captain Clark welcomes you aboard

Glad to have you aboard reader, but remember there is only one captain of this subway – Do not thrust your cock out the train window or beckon lewdly with thy piles nor flush thy beat benny down the drain – (Benny is overcoat in antiquated Times Square argot) – It is forbidden to use the signal rope for frivolous hangings or to burn Nigras in the washroom before the other passengers have made their toilet –

Do not offend the office manager – He is subject to take back the keys of the shit house – Always keep it locked so no sinister stranger sneak a shit and give all the kids in the office some horrible condition – And Mr. Anker from accounting, his arms scarred like a junky from countless Wassermans, sprays plastic over it before he travails there – I stand on the Fifth Amendment, will not answer the question of the Senator from Wisconsin: 'Are you or have you ever been a member of the male sex?' – They can't make Dicky whimper on the boys – Know how I take care of crooners? – Just listen to them – A word to the wise guy – I mean you gotta be careful of politics these days – Some old department get physical with you, kick him right in his coordinator – 'Come see me tonight in my apartment under the school privy – Show you something interesting' said the janitor drooling green coca juice –

The city mutters in the distance pestilent breath of the cancerous librarian faint and intermittent on the warm spring wind –

'Split is the wastings of the cup – Take it away,' he said irritably – Black rocks and brown lagoons invade the world – There stands the deserted transmitter – Crystal tubes click on the message of retreat from the human hill and giant centipedes crawl in the ruined cities of our long home – Thermodynamics has won at a crawl –

'We were caught with our pants down' admits General Patterson 'They rimed the shit out of us.'

Safest way to avoid these horrid perils is come over here and shack up with Scylla – Treat you right, kid – candy and cigarettes –

Woke up in a Turkish Bath under a Johannesberg bidonville

'Where am I you black bastards?'

'Why you junkie white trash rim a shitting Nigger for an eye cup of paregoric!'

dead bird – quail in the slipper – money in the bank – Past port and petal crowned with calm leaves she stands there across the river and under the trees –

Brains spilled in the cocktail lounge – The fat macho has burned down the Jai Lai bookie with his obsidian handled forty five –

shattering bloody blue of Mexico – heart in the sun – pantless corpses hang from telephone poles along the road to Monterrey –

Death rows the boy like sleeping marble down the Grand Canal out into a vast lagoon of souvenir postcards and bronze baby shoes –

'Just build a privy over me, boys' says the rustler to his bunk mates, and the sheriff nods in dark understanding Druid blood stirring in the winds of Panhandle –

Decayed corseted tenor sings Danny Deaver in drag:

'Billy Budd must hang – All hands after to witness this exhibit.'

Billy Budd gives up the ghost with a loud fart and the sail is rent from top to bottom – and the petty officers fall back confounded – 'Billy' is a transvestite liz.

'There'll be a spot of bother about this,' mutters the Master at Arms – The tars scream with rage at the cheating profile in the rising sun –

'Is she dead?'

'So who cares.'

'Are we going to stand still for this? – The officers pull the switch on us,' says young Hassan, ship's uncle –

'Gentlemen,' says Captain Verre 'I cannot find words to castigate this foul and unnatural act whereby a boy's mother take over his body and infiltrate her horrible old substance right onto a decent boat and with bare tits hanging out, unfurls the nastiest colors of the spectroscope.'

A hard-faced matron bandages the cunt of Radiant Jade –

'You see, dearie, the shock when your neck breaks has like an awful effect – You're already dead of course or at least unconscious or at least stunned-but-hu-well-you see – It's a *medical fact* – All your female insides is subject to spurt out your cunt the way it turned the last doctor to stone and we sold the results to Paraguay as a state of Bolivar.'

'I have come to ascertain death not perform a hysterectomy' snapped the old auntie croaker munching a soggy crumpet with his grey teeth – A hanged man plummets through the ceiling of Lord Rivington's smart mews flat – Rivington rings The Home Secretary:

'I'd like to report a leak – '

'Everything is leaking – Can't stem it – Sauve qui peut' snaps The Home Secretary and flees the country disguised as an eccentric lesbian abolitionist –

'We hear it was the other way around, doc,' said the snide reporter with narrow shoulders and bad teeth –

The doctor's face crimsoned 'I wish to state that I have been acting physician at Dankmoor prison for thirty years and always keep my nose clean – Never compromise myself to be alone with the hanged man – Always insist on the presence of my baboon assistant witness and staunch friend in any position.'

Mr. Gilly looks for his brindle-faced cow across the piney woods where armidillos, innocent of a cortex, frolic under the .22 black Stetson and pale blue eyes.

'Lawd Lawd have you seen my brindle-faced cow? – Guess I'm taking up too much of your time – Must be busy doing *something* feller say – Good stand you got whatever it is – Maybe I'm asking too many questions – talking too much – You wouldn't have a rope would you? – A *hemp* rope? Don't know how I'd hold that old brindle-faced cow without a rope if I did come on her – '

phantom riders – chili joints – saloons and the quick draw – hangings from horseback to the jeers of sporting women – black smoke on the hip in the Chink laundry – 'No tickee no washee – Clom Fliday – '

Walking through the piney woods in the Summer dawn, chiggers pinpoint the boy's groin with red dots – smell of boy balls and iron cool in the mouth –

'Now I want you boys to wear shorts,' said the sheriff 'Decent women with telescopes can see you – '

whiff of dried jissom in a bandana rises from the hotel drawer – sweet young breath through the teeth, stomach hard as marble spurts it out in soft, white globs – Funny how a man comes back to something he left in a Peoria hotel drawer 1929 –

1920 tunes drift into the locker room where two boys first time tea high jack off to 'My Blue Heaven' –

In the attic of the big store on bolts of cloth we made it –

'Careful – don't spill – Don't rat on the boys.'

The cellar is full of light – In two weeks the tadpoles hatch – I wonder whatever happened to Otto's boy who played the violin? A hard-faced boy patch over one eye parrot on shoulder says: 'Dead men tell no tales or do they?' – He prods the skull with his cutlass and a crab scuttles out – The boy reaches down and picks up a scroll of hieroglyphs – 'The map! – The map!'

The map turns to shitty toilet paper in his hands blows across a vacant lot in East St. Louis.

The boy pulls off the patch – The parrot flies away into the jungle – Cutlass turns to a machete – He is studying the map and swatting sand flies –

Junk yacks at our heels and predated checks bounce all around us in the Mayan ball court –

'Order in the court – You are accused of soliciting with prehensile piles – What have you to say on your defense?'

'Just cooling them off, judge – raw and bleeding – Wouldn't you?'

'I want you to *smell* this bar stool,' said the paranoid ex-Communist to the manic FBI agent – 'Stink juice, and you may quote me has been applied by paid hoodlums constipated with Moscow goldwasser.'

The man in a green suit – old English cut with two side vents and change pockets outside – will swindle the aging proprietress of a florist shop – 'old flub got a yen on for me – '

carnival of splintered pink peppermint – 'Oh those Golden Slippers' – He sits up and looks into a cobra lamp –

'I am the Egyptian,' he said looking all flat and silly.

And I said: 'Really, Bradford, don't be tiresome – '

Under the limestone cave I met a man with Medusa's head in a hatbox and said 'Be careful' to the customs inspector, freezed his hand forever an inch from the false bottom –

Will the gentle reader get up off his limestones and pick up the phone? – Cause of death: completely uninteresting.

They cowboyed him in the steam room – Is this Cherry Ass Gio the Towel Boy or Mother Gillig Old Auntie of Westminster Place? Only dead fingers talk in braille –

Second run cotton trace the bones of a fix –

But is all back seat dreaming since the hitch-hiker with the chewed thumb and he said: 'If decided? – Could I ride with you chaps?' – (Heard about the death later in a Copenhagen bar – Told a story about crayfish and chased it with a Jew joke out behind the fear of what I tell him we all know here). So it jumped in my throat and was all there like and ready when we were sitting under the pretties, star pretties you understand, not like me talking at all I used to talk differently. Who did? – Paris?

'Mr. Bradly Mr. Martin, Johnny Yenshe, Yves Martin.'

Martin he calls himself but once in the London YMCA on Tottenham Court (never made out there) – once on Dean Street in Soho – No it wasn't Dean Street that was someone else looked like Bradly – It was on some back time street, silent pockets of Mexico City – (half orange with red pepper in the sun) – and the weakness hit me and I leaned against a wall and the white spot never washed out of my glen plaid coat – carried that wall with me to a town in Ecuador can't remember the name, remember the towns all around but not that one where time slipped on the beach – sand winds across the blood – half a cup of water and Martin looked at the guide or was it the other, the Aussie, the Canadian, the South African who is sometimes there when the water is given out and always there when the water gives out – and gave him half his own water ration with gambler fingers could switch water if he wanted to – On the street once Cavesbury Close I think it was somebody called him Uncle Charles in English and he didn't want to know the man walked away dragging one leg –

and I went on about my junk business waiting for the drug store to open the yellow narcotics script in my pocket Place of the Grasshopper all these memories are his old memories digust me to hover around when I took a shot and suddenly say

'I'm absolutely weak I can only just totter home, darling, the dollar has collapsed'

out for the running he can't follow no more . . . fixed his faucet you didn't? . . . He was getting old any case . . . the thirst of Mars . . . sand winds across the blood . . . half a cup of water . . .

'Any number can play?'

I acquiesced in compete passive position I die you die as the case may be out behind the fear of what I tell him we all know here and seen the doctor after the ball pick up the skinned journalist and send the skin home to mother for Christian burial. A careful autopsy of the flayed man revealed he was devoid of an anus venting all waste products from a flexible metal tube which projected from his navel and could be vented through fly sleeve pant leg or cloth hole as the occasion warranted leaving colorless shit in corridors of the world's room shrinking in heavy money. hustling blind streets of score money and back with the gelt score smiled poppies for his lover and loved the stale hotel of Gains' fibrous flesh and the parhafin amours that belonged to the house he bought it and it was his he said . . . but the manikin was unable to confirm the account . . .

'You crazy or something walk around alone?'

The shallow water came in with the tide . . . sick sharks fed on sewage only food of this village . . . swamp delta to the orange sky that does not change . . .

This who is such a devious that I never know for sure whether he does or does not pressure the hotel price . . .

'Doctor, the bunch is out of bounds and over the bread fence.'

'Finnies nous attendons une bonne chance!'

(Last words in the diary of Yves Martin who presumably died of thirst in the Egyptian desert with three companions. Just who died is uncertain since one member of the party has not been found alive or dead and the identity of the missing person is dubious. The bodies were decomposed when found and identification was based on documents clothes and wrist watches. But it seems the party was given to exchange of clothes and documents and even to writing in each other's diaries an unheard of intimacy in any modern expedition.

((("No we do not admit your disputed condition into Lebanon It would jeopardize prominent cedars and undo the good work of Anne Frank."))) Other members of the expedition were Mr. Shanon, Mr. Armstrong, Monsieur Pillou and Ahmed Akid the guide.)

Saw the murder words in the guide's head transparent and I couldn't move back seat dreaming paralyzed like my mother couldn't move paralyzed dream me talk me jack me off from her bed of distant fingers a woman with red hair dead of course her image flashed in the guide's eyes as the wrench fell and I was in the 'bearer' already feeling around to make myself the home the white score, we call it murder words like frantic fish in the shrinking body pool slow motion saw the heavy wrench fall and took the pictures from his eyes in the white flash and the guide did not know he had a hitch hiker until he his knowledge of English summoned more words that he knew and his Arabic only a thin shell around the lodger mud cubicles with blue painted walls his thin black body twisting sodomy shadows from the long mastur- bation nights of Columbus Ohio.

'return various bits and pieces and pitch in with the men.'

'A nice guy myth the bastard dirt mixer.'

'I was a great lover . . . undressed there . . . money . . . good bye . . . and the boys I was this one empty broken very thin standing his underwear ghost spasms slow linen dust freckles hard brown hands I'm selling frayed policy furtive and sad just old nitrous fumes down a funnel of dusty freckles leg through the sad

124

toilet long time not infrequently I stripped to that coin yes boys that's me there by 'Coin a Smell Dorm' photo into a bureau drawer sick rotting pieces opened the gates for you washed face in Panama maybe undressed there washed back on pay of old photo freckle leg here with freckles dusty young hard ons the legs hairs sparse and to the floor intestinal Sad Poison Nice guy you know toilet smell of rain pants.'

'Intestinal Sad Poison Nice Guy' you know 'Toilet Smell of Rain Pants!' 'hands of scar tissue will and brain I hardly breathe faded brown mucous old room . . . cigarette money.'

Not infrequently I stripped to the waist and pitched in with the men yes boys that's me there by the cement mixer

Mr. Bradly Mr. Martin distant fingers in the sick morning rotting pieces of himself dim flickering on the tele from Spain . . . I told him you on tracks . . . couldn't reach me with the knife . . . couldn't switch iron . . . and zero time to the tracks . . . couldn't make turnstile . . . bad shape from death Mr. Shannon no cept

pay of old photo . . . brains burning . . . empty tracks . . . broken boy couldn't . . . couldn't reach me with the knife . . . burning star tracks broken . . . dusty young hard ons . . . excrement winding ghost spasms . . . slow linen to the floor intestinal streets boy's hard brown hands . . . school toilet smell of rain pants hands furtive and sad . . . shit stained comics . . . basement laboratory . . . red nitrous fumes . . . broken dog dragging on rusty cement . . . pensive weasel pain down a funnel of photo faces out in stale streets smell of old pain boy groin pus in the sheets writhing crystal flower leg through the sad toilet slot . . . faded brown mucous old rooming house . . .

return various bits and pieces of the picture that he coin a nice guy myth the bastard dirtier than 'Coin a Smell Dorm . . .' 'I was great lover' He dropped the photo into a bureau drawer 'remember only existence lost I have opened the gates for you . . . sad poison police . . . a sort of compass needle in your brain mouth and nose sealed over . . . boy I was washed face in Panama maybe undressed there. money. good bye.'

'You the great lover to see our worn out film washed back on Spain Repeat Performance page?'

'and the boys I was this one the freckle leg here with freckles very thin standing his underwear thin the leg hairs sparse and glittering dusty freckles from Spain . . . Sad Poison Nice Guy you know I'm selling frayed policy . . . frayed thing of scar tissue neither alive nor dead ... you unfleshed my will and brain. I hardly breathe from his throat smell or feel or see not.'

And there was a blast of a hate from the heavy heart of an old servant 'I am the Director. Mister, leave cigarette money. You have known me for a long time.'

Faded brown smell of carbolic soap and rectal mucous distant 1920 wind and dust.

17

CROSS THE WOUNDED GALAXIES

The penny arcade peep-show long process in different forms.

In the pass the muttering sickness leaped into our throats, coughing and spitting in the silver morning. frost on our bones. Most of the ape-forms died there on the treeless slopes. dumb animal eyes on 'me' brought the sickness from white time caves frozen in my throat to hatch in the warm steamlands spitting. scarlet bursts in egg flesh. beyond the pass, limestone slopes down into a high green savannah and the grass-wind on our genitals. Came to a swamp fed by hot springs and mountain ice. sick apes spitting blood bubbling throats torn with the talk sickness. human faces tentative flicking in and out of focus. We waded into the warm mud-water. hair and ape flesh off in screaming strips. stood naked human bodies covered with phosphorescent green jelly. soft tentative flesh cut with ape wounds. fingers and tongues rubbing off the jelly-cover. body melting pleasure-sounds in the warm mud. till the sun went and a blue wind of silence touched human faces and hair. when we came out of the mud we had names.

names. The sound bubbling in the blood, quivering our throats and swap we had names for each other. tentative flicker-laugh and laughing washed the hairs off. down to his genitals.

And the others did not want to touch me because of the white worm-thing inside but no one could refuse if I wanted and ate the fear-softness in other men. The cold was around us in our bones. And I could see the time before the thing when there was green around the green taste in my mouth and the green plant shit on my legs. before the cold ... And some did not eat flesh and died because they could not live with the thing inside ... Once we caught one of the hairy men with our vine nets and tied him over a slow fire and left him there until he died and the thing sucked his screams moving in my face like smoke and no one could eat the flesh-fear of the hairy man and there was a smell in the cave bent us over ... We moved to keep out of our excrement where white worms twisted up feeling for us and the white worm-sickness in all our bodies. We took our pots and spears and moved South and left the black flesh there in the ashes ... Came to the great dry plain and only those lived who learned to let the thing surface and eat dead animals in the brown water holes ... Then thick grass and trees and animals. I pulled the skin over my head and I made another man put on the skin and horns and we fucked like the animals stuck together and we found the animals stuck together and killed both so I knew the thing inside me would always find animals to feed my mouth meat ... Saw animals chase us with spears and woke eating my own hand and the blood in my mouth made me spit up a bitter green juice. But the next day I ate flesh again and every night we put on animal skins and smeared green animal excrement down our legs and fucked each other with whimpering snorting noises and stuck together shadows on the cave walls, and ate surface men ... The thing inside me would. We caught one of the hairy men animaled him over a slow fire eating my own hand, the thing sucked his screams green bitter juice. Those lived who learned to let the softness in, eat animal excrement in the brown bones ... I made another man put on the skin green plant shit on animals stuck together flesh. So I knew with the thing inside always find animals to feed with our vine nets. Blood in my mouth made me spit up moving in my face like the next day I ate flesh again ... Moved to knee legs and fucked each other twisted up feeling and stuck together shadows on our bodies.

Glass blizzards thru the rusty limestone streets exploded flesh from the laughing bones. spattering blood cross urine of walls. We lived in sewers of the city, crab parasites in our genitals rubbing our diseased flesh thru each other on a long string of rectal mucous. tape-worms with white bone faces and disk mouths feeling for the soft host mucous. the years. the long. the many such a place. In a land of grass without memory, only food of the hordes moving south, the dank armadillo flesh killed in the cool morning grass with throwing sticks. The women and their thing police ate the flesh and we fought over their shit-encrusted pieces of armadillo gristle.

Thru jungles of breath when we copulate with white bone faces. place of nettles and scorpions the cool morning walls. larval bodies feeling the penalty. the years. the long. the many. such shoots growing.

Sitting naked at the bottom of a well the cool mud of evening touched our rectums. We shared a piece of armadillo gristle, eating it out of each other's mouths. above us a dry husk of insect bodies along the stone well-wall and thistles over the well-mouth against green evening sky. licking the gristle from his laughing teeth and gums I said: 'I am Allah. I made you.' A blue mist filled the well and shut off our word-breath. My hands sank into his body. We fell asleep in other flesh. smells on our stomach and hands. woke in noon-sun, thistle shades cutting our soft night flesh.

Evening touched our rectums. mud shells and frogs croaking. licking the gristle asleep with other flesh. the cool mud of breath, and our bodies we shared. branches in the wind. his knees. other mouths. against the green evening sky. 'We laughing teeth and gums,' I said. hands woke in the noon sun soft night flesh. smells on our stomach. thistle shades cutting. penny arcade peep show – long process in different forms – Dead fingers talk in braille.

Think Police keep all Board Room Reports – And we are not allowed to proffer the Disaster Accounts – wind hand caught in the door – explosive bio-advance men out of space to employ electrician in gasoline crack of history – last of the gallant heroes – 'I'm you on tracks, Mr. Bradly Mr. Martin' – couldn't reach flesh in his switch – and zero time to the sick tracks – A long time between suns I held the stale overcoat – sliding between light and shadow – muttering in the dogs of unfamiliar score – cross the wounded galaxies we intersect, poison of dead sun in your brain slowly fading – migrants of ape in gasoline crack of history, explosive bio-advance out of space to neon – 'I'm you, wind hand caught in the door' – Couldn't reach flesh – In sun I held the stale overcoat, Dead Hand stretching the throat – last to proffer the disaster account on tracks. See Mr. Bradly Mr. – '

And being blind may not refuse to hear: Mr. Bradly Mr. Martin, disaster to my blood whom I created' – (The shallow water came in with the tide and the Swedish River of Gothenberg.)

He waves his hand sadly from the soft machine. dead fingers in smoke pointing to Gibraltar.
Jan. 25, Gibraltar.

APPENDIX TO THE SOFT MACHINE

The soft machine is the human body under constant siege from a vast hungry host of parasites with many names but one nature being hungry and one intention to eat.

If I may borrow the lingo of Herr Doctor Freud while continuing to deplore the spread of his couch no one does more harm than folks feel bad about doing it 'Sad Poison Nice Guy' more poison than nice – what Freud calls the 'id' is a parasitic invasion of the hypothalamus and since the function of the hypothalamus is to regulate metabolism . . .

'Only work here me.'

'Under new management.'

What Freud calls the 'super ego' is probably a parasitic occupation of the mid brain where the 'rightness' centers may be located and by 'rightness' I mean where 'you' and 'I' used to live before this 'super ego' moved in room on the top floor if my memory serves. Since the parasites occupy brain areas they are in a position to deflect research from 'dangerous channels'. Apomorphine acts on the hypothalamus to regulate metabolism and its dangers to the parasitic inhabitants of these brain areas can be readily appreciated. You see junk *is* death the oldest 'visitor' in the industry.

A TREATMENT THAT CANCELS ADDICTION

In 1961 I was in contact with a young man of wealth and influence who had just completed the apo-morphine treatment and convinced himself of its unique value in cases of heroin addiction. He assured me that he could draw official attention to this treatment in the United States where the problem of addiction and the number of addicts would form an ideal testing ground for the apo-morphine treatment. At his suggestion in January 1961 Cambridge England I wrote a comprehensive article describing the treatment and its advantages over other methods of treatment in use at the time and unfortunately still in use. The young man is dead now. The nurse who treated him is dead. Doctor Dent is dead now, the London doctor who first started using apo-morphine in the treatment of addictions who used the treatment for 40 years with excellent results as his many cured patients can testify. Doctor Dent was the founder and chairman of *The English Society for the Study of Addictions*. He was in contact with Doctor Isbell of Lexington KY and other workers in the field. Though he tried repeatedly he was never able to interest Doctor Isbell or any of the other doctors connected with the Public Health Service of the United States to give the apo-morphine treatment a trial. I prepared three copies of the original article. One was sent to the young man at whose suggestion the article had been written and reached him shortly before his death. One was lost by a literary agent in New York after being rejected by the Literary Digest and several comparable periodicals – (I should mention in this connection an incident that occurred in 1960 being short of money at the time I accepted a commission from a true detective magazine in the United States to do a piece on 'the corner junky'. Mr. Mellville Hardiment of 6 Cambridge Square prepared the article from notes I provided and I added a page on the apo-morphine treatment. The detectives wrote back that they were taking the article but preferred to omit reference to the apo-morphine treatment since it was a better *story* to leave 'the corner junky' in the gutter where he belongs. I wrote back that their attitude was so inexplicable as to warrant the labels 'unpatriotic' and 'disloyal' disloyal that is to any America or Americans I could consider worthy of loyalty that the possibility of disintoxicating 50,000 miserable addicts was in itself something of a *story*) – The third copy of the article was lost in some remote file but appeared as preface to the Italian version of *Junky* through the good offices of Doctor Pivano Sottsa of Milan. This Italian translation is the only copy of the article that has been published to date. At the time the article was written I did not criticize the American Narcotics Department nor the Public Health Center at Lexington KY I simply suggested that they turn their expensive facilities to the job of disintoxicating 50,000 miserable addicts by the only method of treatment that does the job and if there is one thing America is supposed to stand for it is doing the job. My attempt to attribute good will where it patently does not exist proved ill-advised. The American Narcotics Department has persisted in regarding addiction as criminal in itself with the consequent emphasis on punishment rather than treatment. Addiction is a metabolic illness and no more a police problem that tuberculosis or radium poisoning. Mr. Anschlinger says that the laws against addiction must *reflect* societies disapproval of the addict that is to say *cause* societies disapproval of the addict. Recently when an attempt was made to set up a treatment center in Hoboken the local inhabitants stoned the center screaming 'Are you *high*?' 'Did you bring your *needle*?'

'We will *never* accept criminal men and women in *Hoboken*!'

One sometimes wonders exactly how ugly the ugly American can be and how ill intentioned those who form his so called opinions. Let us look at the record. What has been accomplished by the American Narcotics Department and the Treatment Center at Lexington. The Narcotics Department has indeed as they claim reduced the amount of heroin addicts receive but not the number of addicts. This is an inconsiderable improvement. Whether an addict receives 23 grains of heroin per day or $\frac{1}{4}$ grain he is still an addict and subject to severe withdrawal symptoms if his dose is cut off. In fact addiction can be maintained by as little as one thirtieth of a grain of heroin per day. The incidence of heroin addiction in age groups and social class where it was previously unknown continues to increase. When I was in high school in the 1920s the use of any drug – other than alcohol – was unknown. When I first became addicted to heroin in the 1940s teen aged addicts were still unknown. Now the rising incidence of teen aged addiction has led to extending control measures that have yielded such lamentable results. Addiction is an illness of exposure. One may well ask how were narcotics made available to young people? I can suggest a partial answer to this question. The stringent measures of the American Narcotics Department their vociferous insistence that addiction is a police and not a medical problem spread the infection. In the 1920s and 30s heroin was much more readily available than it is now *to those already addicted*. Pusher sold to addicts and most of their business came from the seedy furtive small time underworld short change artists thieves pimps and whores. It was a world of shabby streets and rooming houses far removed from high school students. At that time it was quite easy to support a morphine habit from doctor's prescriptions and many of the old itinerant con men used this route exclusively. When the American Narcotics Department berserk with Parkinson's Law began a program of wholesale arrest and disproportionate sentences for possession many of the old time addicts and pushers were put out of circulation. Some old-timers quit in disgust. Even the Mafia decided there are safer and easier ways to make money. As a result a whole new generation of users and pushers arose. This new generation of pushers turned to the teen aged market. This development was easy to foresee by any person with a clear mind. I am saying that the American Narcotics Department *deliberately* spread the illness of addiction to young people? Whether an agent acts deliberately or not is about as interesting as how many angels can dance on the point of a pin. By their fruits you will know them and the fruits of the American Narcotics Department are deplorable. This brings us to the possibility of quarantining or containing the illness of addiction which has been the English system – (This article is *not* an argument for introducing the English system into the United States) – In England a doctor may prescribe any amount of heroin for an addicted patient but will not prescribe unless he has satisfied himself the patient is already addicted. Since heroin is available to an addict legally and he can buy it at drug store prices he does not need to buy on the black market though admittedly an addict may sell off a pill or two from his allowance to other addicts. The number of addicts in the United Kingdom is estimated at 600 as opposed to 50,000 addicts in the United States. Recently pressure from American sources has been brought to bear on England and there is talk of changing the system. English doctors are opposed to the change since they feel it will give police officers the right to tell a doctor what he can and cannot prescribe. This right has long been vested in the American Narcotics Department and a doctor may lose his licence if he prescribes for addicts. The policies of the American Narcotics Department are not calculated to contain but to spread the illness of addiction. They have not reduced the number of those affected. They say themselves that addiction is on the increase especially among young people. The pretext of looking for narcotics gives them the right to search any person or premises at any time. The Department is continually lobbying for more anti-narcotic laws and stiffer penalties. Many of the laws passed under this pressure are very dangerous indeed to our so called freedom. In Louisiana and California it is a felony *to be* an addict. Penalizing a state of being apart from any proven illegal act sets a precedent that could be extended to other categories of 'offenders' including anyone opposed to official policies. To classify all opposition as criminal is of course the simple device by which a Fascist regime takes over and proclaims a majority. In December of 1964 I returned to the States and was detained three hours at customs while narcotics agents read my notes letters and diary. Finding no narcotics they then informed me I was subject to fine and imprisonment for failing to register with the Department when I left the country and for failing to inform the customs officer of my narcotics record on my return. The law requiring addicts to register only applies to those who have been convicted under federal state or city violations of the Harrison Narcotics Act or the Marijuana Act of 1937. I have been arrested twice in the United States once 17 years ago and once 20 years ago. In neither case was I convicted. In any case this law would seem to make it a crime *ever to have been* an addict.

Now let us look at the Treatment Center at Lexington. What treatment is given? A ten day reduction cure with methodone yielding almost unanimous relapse at the first opportunity as the doctors at Lexington readily admit. The head of the research department at Lexington is Doctor Isbell. Doctor Dent was never able to interest him in the apo-morphine treatment though Doctor Isbell has seen the results. I know of one occasion when he talked with two of Doctor Dent's cured patients. He told Doctor Dent that he considered the treatment too dangerous. Dangerous to who? Experiments at Lexington seem oriented towards establishing the addictive liability of decorticated canine preparations! Yes even a dog with its brains cut out can be hooked. I could have told you that before you stuck the needle in doc. The treatment at Lexington is now six months of confinement after the initial ten day reduction with substitute drugs. Public health officials now wish to extend this period saying that prolonged involuntary confinement is necessary because the addict does not 'want' to be cured. Of course addicts do not 'want' to be cured since it is precisely the centers of 'wanting' that have been taken over by the drug. When they begin to lose the need for morphine in the course of the apo-morphine treatment many will 'want' to continue the treatment and stay off drugs. The apo-morphine treatment takes about 8 to 10 days. After treatment the cured addict finds that he can resist relapse. Apo-morphine precisely activates the resistance centers. In 1959 a heavily subsidized magazine called The Western World published an article called Fighting Drug Addiction. I typed out selections from this article and cut the page into four sections rearranging the sections. A surprisingly clear and far-sighted statement as to the aims and methods of the American Narcotics Department emerges from the scissors. I submit the rearranged text with corroborative items that appeared in 1965.

PLAN DRUG ADDICTION

Now you are asking me whether I want to perpetuate a narcotics problem and I say: 'Protect the disease. *Must be made criminal* protecting society from the disease.'

The problem scheduled in the United States the use of jail, former narcotics plan, addiction and crime for many years – broad front 'care' of welfare agencies – narcotics which antedate the use of drugs – The fact is noteworthy – 48 stages – prisoner was delayed – has been separated – was required.

Addiction in some form is the basis – must be wholly addicts – *Any voluntary capacity subversion of the* Will Capital and Treasury Bank – Infection dedicated to traffic in exchange narcotics demonstrated a Typhoid Mary who will spread narcotics problem to the United Kingdom – Finally in view of the cure of the social problem and as such dangerous to society – Release the prosecutor to try any holes.

Cut up Fighting Drug Addiction by Malcolm Monroe Former Prosecutor in *Western World*, October, 1959.

And here is an item that appeared six years later May 3, 1965 in the New York Journal American.

JAIL MAY BE BEST RX FOR ADDICTS MD SAYS

The specialist doctor George E. Vaillant, a psychiatrist at the United States Public Health Service in Lexington KY, said: 'The likelihood that significant abstinence would occur after *prolonged involuntary imprisonment* followed by *prolonged involuntary supervision* is say 15 times greater than after voluntary hospitalization.' He adds that delinquency addiction, broken homes and slum residence are probably interdependent.

There is a general feeling in America that officials must be doing the right thing a feeling that the officials in question take good pains to foster. Why they should be listened to when what they say adds up neither to good sense or good intentions is difficult to understand. If the official agencies have failed to solve the narcotics problem or to state it honestly the non-official agencies have done little better. Recently centers of treatment have sprung up where the addicts receive no other medication than prayer. This inspirational and quasi-religious approach to a metabolic illness is ill advised. It would be equally logical to prescribe prayer for malaria. Recently in New York doctors have been allowed to prescribe methodone for heroin addicts. Heroin addicts lose the desire for heroin in the course of this treatment. Over a period of five years they hope to reduce the dosage of methodone. Methodone is an opiate stronger than morphine and quite as addictive. To say that addicts have been cured of heroin by the use of methodone is like saying an alcoholic has been cured of whisky by the use of gin. If the addicts lose their desire for heroin it is because the methodone dosage is stronger than the diluted heroin they receive from pushers.

Junk is a generic term for all habit forming preparations and derivatives of opium including the synthetics: morphine, heroin, dilaudid, codeine, dio-codeine, dihidro-codeine, demerol, methodone, palfium to give partial list. There are also non-habit forming derivatives and preparations of opium. Papaverene which is found in raw opium is non-habit forming. Apo-morphine which is derived from morphine is non-habit forming. Yet both substances are classified as narcotics under the Harrison Narcotics Act. Not only does Congress propose to create gentlemen and criminals by act of Congress but also to alter the physiological action of drugs. Any form of junk can cause addiction. Nor does it make much difference whether it is injected sniffed or taken orally. The result is always the same – addiction. The addict functions on junk. Like a diver depends on his junk line. When his junk is cut off he suffers agonizing withdrawal symptoms: watering burning eyes, light fever, hot and cold flashes, leg and stomach cramps, diarrhoea, insomnia, prostration, in some cases death from circulatory collapse and shock. Withdrawal symptoms are distinguished from any syndrome of comparable severity by the fact that they are immediately relieved by administering a sufficient quantity of opiates. The withdrawal symptoms reach their peak on the fourth day then gradually disappear over a period of three to six weeks. The later stages of withdrawal are marked by profound depression. The exact mechanisms of addiction are not known. Doctor Isbell has suggested that junk blankets the cell receptors. This cell blanketing action could account both for the pain killing and the habit forming action of junk. Certainly the mechanism by which junk relieves pain. The way in which junk relieves pain is habit forming and all preparations of junk so far tested have proved habit forming to the extent of their effectiveness as pain killers. Any preparation of junk that relieves acute pain will afford proportionate relief to withdrawal symptoms. A non-habit forming morphine would seem to be a latter day philosopher's stone yet much of the research at Lexington is currently oriented in this barren direction. When the cell blanketing agent is removed the body undergoes an agonizing period of reconversion to normal metabolism characterized by the withdrawal symptoms already described.

The question as to what sort of persons become addicts has been answered by the Public Health Department: 'Anyone who takes any addicting preparation long enough.' The time necessary to establish addiction varies with individual susceptibility and the addictive strength of the preparation used. Normally anyone who receives daily injections totalling one grain of morphine every day for a month will experience considerable discomfort if the injections are discontinued. Four to six months of use is enough to establish full addiction. Addiction is an illness of exposure. By and large those become addicts who have access to junk. In Iran where opium was sold openly in shops they had three million addicts. There is no more a pre-addict personality than there is a pre-malarial personality – all the hogwash of psychiatry to the contrary. (Parenthetically it is my opinion that 9 out of 10 psychiatrists should be broken down to veterinarians and their books called in for pulping). To say it country simple most folks enjoy junk. Having once experienced this pleasure the human organism will tend to repeat it and repeat it and repeat it. The addict's illness *is* junk. Knock on any door. Whatever answers the door give it four ½ grain shots of God's Own Medicine every day for six months and the so called 'addict personality' is there . . . an old junky selling Christmas seals on North Clark St. the 'Priest' they called him seedy and furtive cold fish eyes that seem to be looking at something other folks can't see. That something he is looking at is junk. The whole addict personality can be summed up in one sentence: *The addict needs junk.* He will do a lot to get junk just as you would do a lot for water if you were thirsty enough. You see junk *is* a personality a seedy grey man couldn't be anything else but junk rooming house a shabby street room on the top floor these stairs/cough/the 'Priest' there pulling himself up along the banister bathroom yellow wood panels dripping toilet works stached under the wash basin back in his room now cooking up grey shadow on a distant wall used to be me Mister. I was on junk for almost fifteen years. In that time I took ten cures. I have been to Lexington and took the reduction scored for paregoric in Cincinnati the day after I got out dressed in my banker suit and carrying The Wall Street Journal

'It's my wife she uh . . .'

'I quite understand sir. Would you like the two ounce family size?'

'Why yes I believe so.'

I have taken abrupt withdrawal treatments and prolonged withdrawal treatments, cortisone, tranquillizers, anti-histamines and the prolonged sleep cure. In every case I relapsed at the first opportunity. Why do addicts voluntarily take a cure and then relapse? I think on a deep biological level most addicts want to be cured. Junk *is* death and your body knows it. I relapsed because I was never physiologically cured until I took the apo-morphine treatment. Apo-morphine is the only agent I know that evicts the 'addict personality', my old friend Opium Jones. We were mighty close in Tangier 1957 shooting every hour 15 grains of methodone per day which equals 30 grains of morphine and that's a lot of GOM. I never changed my clothes. Jones likes his clothes to season in stale rooming house flesh until you can tell by a hat on the table, a coat hung over a chair that Jones lives there. I never took a bath. Old Jones don't like the feel of water on his skin. I spent whole days looking at the end of my shoe just communing with Jones. Then one day I saw that Jones was not a real friend, that our interests were in fact divergent. So I took a plane to London and found Doctor Dent charcoal fire in the grate Scottish terrier cup of tea. He told me about the treatment and I entered the nursing home the following day. It was one of those four storey buildings on Cromwell Road room with rose wall paper on the third floor. I had a day nurse and a night nurse and received an injection of apo-morphine one twentieth grain every two hours day and night. Doctor Dent told me I could have morphine if I needed it but the amount would be small ¼ grain per shot for the first 24 hours and after that one eighth grain – one twelfth what I had been using quite a cut again the next day.

Now every addict has his special symptom, the one that hits him hardest when his junk is cut off. With me it's *feeling* the slow painful death of Mr. Jones. Listen to the old timers in Lexington talking about their symptom:

'Now with me it's puking is the worst.'

'I never puke. It's this cold burn on my skin drives me up the wall.'

'My trouble is sneezing.'

'I feel myself encased in the old grey corpse of Mr. Jones. Not another person in this world I want to see. Not a thing I want to do except revive Mr. Jones.'

Third day cup of tea at dawn calm miracle of apo-morphine. I was learning to live without Jones reading newspapers writing letters most cases I can't write a letter for a month and here I was writing a letter on the third day and looking forward to a talk with Doctor Dent who isn't Jones at all. Apo-morphine had taken care of my special symptom. Seven days after entering the nursing home I got my last eighth grain shot. Three days later I left the hospital. I went back to Tangier where junk was readily available at that time. I didn't have to use will power whatever that is. I just didn't want any junk. The apo-morphine treatment had given me a long calm look at all the grey junk yesterdays a long calm look at Mr. Jones standing there in his shabby black suit and grey felt hat stale rooming house flesh cold undersea eyes. So I boiled him in hydrochloric acid. Only way to get him clean you understand layers and layers of that grey junk rooming house smell.

Apo-morphine is made from morphine by boiling with hydrochloric acid but its physiological action is quite different. Morphine sedates the front brain. Apo-morphine stimulates the back brain and the vomiting centers. One twelfth grain of apo-morphine injected will produce vomiting in a few minutes and for many years the only use made of this drug was as an emetic in cases of poisoning.

When Doctor Dent started using the apo-morphine treatment 40 years ago all his patients were alcoholics. He would put a bottle of whisky by the bed and invite the patient to drink all he wanted. But with each drink the patient received an injection of apo-morphine. After a few days the patient conceived such a distaste for alcohol that he would ask to have the bottle removed from the room. Doctor Dent thought at first that this was due to a conditioned aversion since the spirit was associated with a dose of apo-morphine that often produced vomiting. However he found that some of his patients were not in the least nauseated by the dose of apo-morphine received – There is considerable individual variation – None the less these patients experienced the same distaste for alcohol and voluntarily stopped drinking after a few days of treatment. He concluded that his patients conceived a distaste for alcohol because they no longer needed it and that apo-morphine acts on the back brain to regulate metabolism so that the body no longer needs a sedative to which it has become accustomed. From that time he stressed the fact that apo-morphine *is not an aversion treatment*. Apo-morphine is a *metabolic regulator* and is the only drug known that acts in this way to normalize a disturbed metabolism.

The treatment is fully described with dosage in Doctor Dent's book *Anxiety And Its Treatment* published by Sheffington in London. Anyone undertaking to administer the apo-morphine treatment should consult this book. It is essential to the success of the treatment to give sufficient quantity of apo-morphine over a sufficient period of time. If the apo-morphine is given by injection one twentieth grain should be injected every two hours day and night for the first four days. Some people are more sensitive to apo-morphine than others and find this dose too nauseating. Since apo-morphine works by regulating metabolism and not by aversion nausea and vomiting should be avoided whenever possible. If the method of administration is sublingual as much as a tenth of a grain can be given every hour. With sublingual administration it is quite easy to control or eliminate nausea and the entire treatment can be carried out successfully without a single instance of vomiting. *The concentration of apo-morphine in the system must reach a certain level for the treatment to be successful.* I have known doctors in America who gave two injections of apo-morphine per day. This is quite worthless. It is important to remember that any opiate or any sedative reverses the action of apo-morphine. So if any opiates are given, and this will only be necessary in cases of heavy addiction, it is essential to continue the injections of apo-morphine for at least 24 hours after the last injection of opiates. As regards sedatives, tranquillizers and sleeping pills absolutely none should be given.

Admittedly the treatment of 50,000 addicts would be expensive but we are already spending millions of dollars on programs of treatment and control that do not work. If the program is properly presented many addicts will report voluntarily for treatment. Those who volunteer for treatment are the best prospects and will provide an ever increasing number of testimonials to its success. If the addict is informed that he will get junk if he needs it he will be much more willing to undergo treatment. Tincture of opium or a drug like dio-codeine given orally would be preferable to injections. Administering the apo-morphine sublingually would cut down personal requirement and minimize the incidence of nausea. Music through head phones provides considerable relief during withdrawal and this should be provided. The treatment is from 5 to 10 days depending on the degree of addiction. The treatment should be followed by 20 days rest in the hospital. At the end of a month patients could be discharged and given a prescription for oral apo-morphine tablets to use in case of relapse. Apo-morphine is completely non-habit forming and no case of addiction to apo-morphine has ever been recorded. It is a metabolic regulator and not a sedative. Once it has done its work of regulating the metabolism its use can be discontinued. There is no kick to apo-morphine and no one would take it for pleasure. Like a good policeman apo-morphine does its work and goes. The fact that apo-morphine *is not* an addictive substitute drug is crucial. In any reduction cure the addict knows that he is still receiving narcotics and he dreads the time when the last dose is withdrawn. In the

141

apo-morphine treatment the addict know he is getting better *without* morphine.

I feel that any form of so called psychotherapy is strongly contra-indicated for addicts. Addicts should not be led to dwell on or relive the addict experience since this conduces to relapse. The question 'Why did you start using narcotics in the first place?' should never be asked. It is quite as irrelevant to treatment as it would be to ask a malarial patient why he went to a malarial area.

Apo-morphine has proved useful in the treatment of other addictions and chronic intoxications: barbiturates, chloral, amphetamine. There are thousands of barbiturate addicts in the United States and the treatment of this addiction is even more difficult and time consuming than the treatment of heroin addiction. The withdrawal of barbiturates must be effected very slowly and under constant supervision. Otherwise the addict is subject to convulsive seizures that can result in serious injuries. Barbiturate addicts treated with apo-morphine can be cut off barbiturates *immediately* without convulsions or other serious symptoms. Barbiturate addicts suffer from severe insomnia during withdrawal and it may be some weeks before the sleep cycle is normalized. Treated with apo-morphine they sleep normally. Amphetamine users on the other hand often fall into such a deep sleep when the drug is cut off they cannot be aroused to eat. Treated with apo-morphine they sleep normally and can be easily aroused. This brings us once again to the unique value of apo-morphine as a drug that normalizes metabolism which would indicate its use in conditions other than addiction. Doctor Feldman of Switzerland has noted that in cases showing an excess of chloresterol in the blood this condition disappeared after treatment with apo-morphine. Doctor Xavier Coore of Paris told me recently that he finds apo-morphine an extremely useful drug in general practice. He prescribes apo-morphine for anxiety, grief, nervousness, insomnia in short for all the conditions where tranquillizers and barbiturates are usually given. Certainly it is a much safer drug since there is no danger of addiction or even dependence. When you take apo-morphine for a severe emotional state you have faced the problem not avoided it. The apo-morphine has normalized your metabolism always disturbed in any emotional upset so that you can face the problem with calmness and sanity. Apo-morphine is the *anti anxiety* drug. I have witnessed in others and experienced myself dramatic relief from anxiety caused by mescalin after a dose of apo-morphine where tranquillizers were quite ineffective.

A number of addicts have taken the apo-morphine treatment at my suggestion. All agreed that it is the only treatment that works and also the least painful form of treatment. Yet most American doctors are completely ignorant of its use in treating addictions. The Merx Index lists apo-morphine as a 'dangerous depressant'. As a matter of fact few drugs are less dangerous. Apo-morphine is only contra-indicated in the special conditions where vomiting is dangerous. Apo-morphine is listed as a narcotic in the United States and subject to the same regulations as morphine and heroin with regard to prescription and use. In both France and England apo-morphine is not on the dangerous drug list. A doctor's prescription is required but the prescription can be filled and refilled any number of times. It is difficult to avoid the conclusion that deliberate attempt has been made in the United States to mislead medical opinion and minimize the value of the apo-morphine treatment. *No variation of the apo-morphine formula has ever been manufactured and the formula has never been synthesized.* With synthesis and variation the side effect of vomiting could probably be eliminated and drugs developed exerting ten or fifty times the regulatory action of the existing preparation. These drugs could excise from the planet what we call anxiety. Since all monopolistic and hierarchical systems are basically rooted in anxiety it is not surprising that the use of the apo-morphine treatment or the synthesis of the apo-morphine formula have been consistently opposed in certain drearily predictable quarters of the soft machine.